EXTREME ACTION

It was Ran's turn to get angry. "So what? I should worry about some old Nazi when there are Arabs running all over Europe trying to kill our people? This is something in the past, something *your* generation remembers. Ask anyone my age if they ever heard of Wagner. Bormann, maybe. Eichmann, yes. Go out in the goddamn street and ask the first ten people you see who Heinz Wagner is. They just don't know. And you want to steer me off the people who are trying to kill us today to look for some doddering old fool from thirty years ago?"

THE EICHMANN SYNDROME

URI DAN
& Edward Radley

LEISURE BOOKS • NEW YORK CITY

A LEISURE BOOK

Published by
Nordon Publications, Inc.
Two Park Avenue
New York, N.Y. 10016

Copyright © 1977 by Nordon Publications, Inc.

THE EICHMANN SYNDROME

Chapter One

The guidebook said the Piazza Navona in the center of historic Rome was worth a special journey. Sam Goldhill sat back on the cafe terrace and tried to take it all in. The book said that nineteen hundred years ago it was a stadium built by the Emperor Domitian who used to flood it and stage mock battles between seagoing galleys rowed by slaves—"and I bet a few of those slaves were Jews," thought Goldhill. Now as the sun scorched down in mid-July there was no trace of the old stadium except its boat-like shape, pointed at the "bows" and square at the "stern." In the center of the square was the massive Fountain of the Rivers with four statues representing the Nile, the Danube, the Ganges and the Plate, incorporating a built-in insult by the fountain's architect Gian Lorenzo Bernini to his arch-rival Francesco Borromini. When Bernini built his fountain in 1651 he saw to it that the statue of the River Plate had a look of horror on his face and an arm raised above his head. The arm was to ward off the concave façade of the Church of Sant'Agnese in Agone, built around the same time by Borromini, which Bernini swore was about to collapse.

As Goldhill could see, the joke was on Bernini. The façade was still there, and the River Plate was still braced for impact.

A few hairy hippie horrors were dabbling their filthy feet in the fountain and one girl was even trying to wash some rags she presumably regarded as clothing, until a Roman cop won the slow-race walking over to her from the shade to tell her to get lost. As the girl turned out to be Italian, and as any order given by an Italian policeman is considered by Italians to be a basis for discussion, a screaming match ensued.

Goldhill sighed, half closed his eyes, and tried to picture the old Roman war galleys sailing round the square, but his reverie was interrupted by a pair of teenagers howling by on motor scooters with the exhaust pipe mufflers sawn off to produce the maximum noise. And the Piazza was supposed to be a traffic-free island.

The cop took no notice and unconcerned Italians sitting at the next table went on sucking away at the mind-jolting dark stains in the bottom of their cups called "espressos." What the guide book did not tell Goldhill was that Rome was Italy's noisiest city, but after a week there he had begun to guess it.

His eyes wandered down to his lap, covered by a piece of wet white cloth. The waiter had sworn it was a napkin but it felt more like a poultice. He remembered a phrase from a previous visit—was it "as damp as a Roman napkin" or "as Roman as a damp napkin?" Either way, it had to be because the cheapskate restaurateur used the same set for both dinner and lunch. If the sun didn't shine between meals in the mornings and afternoons the customers could count on vanishing trouser creases, and maybe a touch of arthritis.

Goldhill, heavy-lidded with the heat, looked out at the square again and saw some kids clustered around the balloon man who had just arrived. Every afternoon the balloon man showed up, gray-haired, unshaven and shabbily dressed, to sell his balloons inflated from a

8

hydrogen cylinder. They sold for two hundred lire plain or two hundred and fifty lire decorated with a rabbit face and ears. In the week Goldhill had been coming to the Piazza for lunch, or a coffee at night, the balloon man had always arrived. At night his best customers were the Italian cafe creepers who used to buy a balloon and pop it behind one of the dozens of passing foreign girl tourists. Goldhill had seen the trick work time and again, with the city gigolo taking the startled girl off to a meal for which she would have to pay in the end when 'Andsome Antonio suddenly realized he had forgotten his wallet.

One night a bunch of crocked Englishmen had bought forty balloons from the man, tied them all together on a long piece of string and launched them "to the moon." They got stuck at the top of the Sant'Agnese in Agone façade, and the drunks started buying more.

The tall, eagle-faced balloon man, who only spoke to give the price of his balloons and who stared out of steely gray eyes, allowed himself a slight change of expression that night. Goldhill suddenly realized the man had been smiling—and not a particularly pleasant smile at that.

As he thought back on the incident and stared at the shirt-sleeved, baggy-trousered balloon man, Goldhill suddenly became aware of an intrusive noise even more persistent than the screaming hippies and the passing motor scooters. A woman's voice was saying: "Sam, Sam, did you hear what I said?"

Goldhill's eyes suddenly focused on the handsome dark-eyed woman sitting next to him, and remembered he was sitting there on holiday with his wife.

It was strange the way they had married several years before. He had thought he would never get married to anyone, let alone Miriam. There he had been, paunchy, comfortable, the wrong side of forty, minding his own business in a superbly appointed bachelor flat in Hampstead. On weekends it was golf, an occasional trip water-skiing in the South of France and some of the gentler slopes in the Alps. On these trips more than enough pretty young girls had been willing to keep him company. His clothing business was running itself by now and he had been looking forward to a life of ease and perpetual bachelordom with an efficient if flinty housekeeper and an XJ-12 in the garage below.

That was before his dear mother started working him over. He was the only boy. His father was dead after his mother had more or less badgered him into the grave and collected a handsome estate and a hefty insurance policy. She had nothing better to do than bug her son.

As he dutifully reported for dinner every Friday night at her Golders Green home, the conversation invariably came round to the same thing.

"You should marry, Sam. It's no good you running round with all those flighty gentile girls. You'll be lonely later, as I am now." Out came a handkerchief and a sob at this point. "You should find a nice Jewish girl to look after you, and you should have some children."

No doubt his mother fancied herself in the grandmother role, regardless of the fact that he could not stand other people's children and had no reason to suspect he would particularly like his own.

Another tack had been: "Sam, you do like girls, don't you? I mean," with an anxious look, "there's nothing wrong, is there?"

Goddamit, thought Goldhill, my own mother trying to make me out a fag. "I'm sorry, mother. I'm happy the way I am. I have plenty of friends and I don't happen to know any nice Jewish girls I want to marry this week."

His mother took what she thought was the hint. Every Friday after that she paraded before him an endless string of Jewish girls, mostly the daughters of his late father's colleagues, whom mother considered "suitable." Goldhill bore it all with reasonably good grace. But his sales resistance remained firm and his marital status seemed assured—single.

But about five years ago he had been caught in a weak moment. He had just had a row with a bunny girl he was rather fond of and had known for some months, and she had walked out on him. Goldhill wasn't used to that kind of treatment. He liked to set the farewell scenes himself, with an expensive quiet dinner, a costly *cadeau de rupture*, and always leaving open the possibility of calling again "for old time's sake" if he felt like it. Or he would pass a girl on to some other lecher at the club. But this stupid cow had actually had the nerve to walk out on him, to claim she had been having it off and away with another fellow and to throw a diamond brooch he had given her on the floor as she stalked out of his bachelor pad.

Sam Goldhill's pride was badly hurt.

He was going through a phase of wanting nothing to do with empty-headed dolly-birds when he met Miriam at a cocktail party. She was slender, attractive, in her mid-thirties and recovering from a broken first marriage to a business acquaintance of his.

Both on the rebound, they had married within weeks, much to his mother's surprise and delight.

Now she was talking to him on the Piazza Navona.

"Sorry, dear," mumbled Goldhill. "I couldn't hear because of those damned motor scooters."

"I said that balloon man looks just like Heinz Wagner."

Goldhill's heart sank at the words, for he had heard them many times before.

Miriam had a fixation which had haunted her throughout her life. The daughter of German Jews, she and her parents had been arrested as war clouds loomed in 1938 and taken to one of the concentration camps whose existence was only rumored in those days. Miriam's two uncles had seen the warning light before her father and had fled to England several years previously.

The commandant of the camp Miriam had been in was a horrifying young SS Major named Heinz Wagner whose devotion to wiping out the Jews had earned him rapid promotion throughout the SS ranks and a top place at the Nuremberg trials, with a death sentence pronounced in absentia.

In the pre-war days, a bribe in the right place could still do something. Jews were prepared to pay vast ransoms to the Germans to get their relatives out of the camps. In Miriam's case, her two uncles in Britain had been trying to get the whole family out of Germany.

But there was only enough money to buy Miriam, then six years old.

Forever she would remember the last time she saw her parents. She clung to her mother and father as a Swiss Red Cross official waited for her at the camp gates. Her parents' tears flowed uncontrollably as they made a promise they knew they could never fulfill to join her very soon.

Standing nearby was Wagner, who finally stalked over and wrenched her father away. "Don't worry," he leered down into the child's face. "I am going to take very good personal care of your mother and father — very good care."

He burst into laughter as the little girl was led to a waiting truck. The last thing she remembered was looking over her shoulder at Wagner, who was laughing, and then seeing him turn and strike her father across the face with his riding crop.

Miriam had arrived in England via Switzerland, and there her uncles had brought her up.

She never saw her parents again.

And she never forgot Wagner's face.

Before Goldhill married Miriam, she had told him of those dark days. But it was not until after they were married that she told him she carried a photograph of Wagner everywhere with her in the hope that somewhere one day she would see him and denounce him.

Now she had the faded photograph in her hand again and was staring at the balloon man.

Goldhill shuddered at moments like this.

Miriam had persuaded him to take her to Germany on holiday a few years ago. He had been reluctant, and rightly so.

While they were there, Miriam had been tense all the time, ready to take abrupt German manners as a personal insult, convinced that everyone was Wagner. There had been a hotel manager and even a restaurant waiter.

There must have been thousands of other concentration camp inmates all over the world doing the same thing.

At each "sighting" Goldhill had been patiently able to convince his wife that she had not finally come face to face with her parents' executioner.

Here we go again, thought Goldhill, but he said aloud mildly: "You know, I think Wagner must be dead by now. You shouldn't disturb yourself like this all the time."

"I don't believe it," said Miriam. "You know he deliberately tried to make it look as if he were dead after the war. When they dug his grave up they found three bodies, none of them his."

Goldhill knew it all right. He knew it by heart. Besides the photograph of Wagner she carried an old French magazine clipping she had come across in Paris one day. It marked the anniversary of VE day, the end of the war in Europe. The magazine had been doing one of those "Where Are They Now?" features on all the missing Nazi war criminals. There was the usual bit on Eichmann, the one the Israelis had smuggled back to trial and execution from Argentina, and the Rogues' Gallery of the men still presumed at large—Bormann, Mueller, Mengele, Wagner and others.

Goldhill reached over and took the magazine clipping and picture.

Wagner had made Colonel by the end of the war and he was a man the Jews particularly wanted to "help them with their inquiries." The way the Jewish and other survivors of the concentration camps told it, Wagner made Ilse Koch—that charming lady who made lampshades out of human skin—look like Florence Nightingale. The War Crimes Commission, the Germans, the Israelis and several other agencies "credited" Wagner with supervising the death of a quarter of a million Jews and Poles in various concentration camps under direct orders from Eichmann. Among his other services to the Thousand Year Reich he had devised a money-saving system by which only half the gas normally used in the gas chambers was injected, prolonging the agony and ensuring panic inside the chambers so that the condemned literally trampled each other to death as they tried hopelessly to batter their way to freedom and the last to survive choked slowly in the remaining fumes.

On a dull evening, just for kicks, he would select a few male prisoners at random and squeeze their genitals to a pulp in a carpenter's vice.

Women prisoners who still seemed attractive despite their skeletal condition would be raped by the good colonel before red hot pokers were jammed into their genitalia, as he chortled, "I may not be the first, but by God, I'm the last."

Colonel Wagner was always described as the life and soul of any party by his fellow officers, always ready to think up a new "show" at the camps to brighten the long winter nights, such as hanging prisoners up by their thumbs with piano wire and placing small bets on which prisoner would hang the longest before his weight pulled him down and stripped the skin off his thumbs.

A number of people were interested in hearing Wagner tell it like it had been.

According to the magazine Goldhill was reading (he could read French even if he couldn't speak more than enough to order a meal), Wagner, if he was still alive, had taken a lot of trouble to make it look as if he were dead.

The article added: "He was a great friend of Himmler and his Gestapo chief Heinrich Mueller, overlords of the world's most deadly and efficient police force at the end of the war. The Gestapo destroyed all records of Wagner's fingerprints during the last days of the Nazi collapse. In May 1947, American Intelligence men were told that Wagner's body had been found in the ruins of Berlin and buried in a cemetery in the suburbs of the city. The tombstone bore the inscription: 'To our dear father Heinz Wagner, killed in action May 1945.' Eighteen years later the grave was opened up. The bones of three people were found in it—none of them Wagner's."

There was a big front-face head and shoulders picture of Wagner, too.

And that was all.

Goldhill looked up at the balloon man again. He was much older than the picture in the magazine, but then he would have to be at least thirty years older. Wagner was only thirty-seven at the end of the war. If he were alive today he would be about sixty-seven. The balloon man looked sixty-seven. Wagner had a long aquiline nose. The balloon man had a long aquiline nose. Wagner had a black hairline starting high on his forehead. The balloon man had a white hairline starting high on his forehead.

Wagner's ears stuck out at the side. The balloon man had jug ears too.

Goldhill looked at Miriam and said patiently, "Look, dear, you can't just have a coincidence like that. You can't come here, sit down for lunch and there in front of you is a man everyone's been looking for since the war. Things just don't happen that way."

Miriam put her hand on his and said very quietly: "Sam, I know I was wrong in Germany and that time in Paris —but just look at that man and this picture. Does he look like it or not?"

"Well yes, he does, but he's older and thinner and I bet the top Nazis salted away a lot of money in case they lost. If Wagner's alive he'll be living the life of Riley down in South America just like the rest of them. He won't be selling balloons on Rome streetcorners."

"So what about his boss Eichmann? When the Israelis found him he was working as a broken-down mechanic and living in a crummy flat. He didn't have any money that anyone knew about. He was doing the best he could. If Eichmann had to live that way, what about his former underlings?"

Goldhill hated to admit it, but his wife was speaking with deadly logic for a change. It was all just too ridiculous, too much of a coincidence, like winning the top prize in a football pool at the first try.

Goldhill handed the magazine back to his wife and carefully dropped his wet napkin on the straw seat beside him before standing up.

"What are you going to do?"

"I am going," said Goldhill, "to buy you a balloon."

Slowly he walked the twenty-five yards to the balloon man and stood waiting as some children carefully selected their balloons and the hawker inflated each one from his hydrogen cylinder. Still in the gas business, though Goldhill. The man seemed to be about an inch taller than Goldhill's five feet eleven. When he looked up, Goldhill noticed the cold gray-eyed stare again. *"Quanti?"* asked the balloon man curtly.

"Just two," said Goldhill in English, although he could have managed the Italian for two, *due*.

The man pulled out two balloons and started blowing them up. Well, thought detective Goldhill, nothing in that. With all the tourists who come around here he can probably understand all the numbers up to ten in at least five languages. Anyway this guy was supposed to be a Kraut, not an Englishman.

Goldhill tried again. "It's a lovely day."

The man finished tying up the balloons, handed them to Goldhill and held out his hand.

"Cinquecento."

The man's no fool, thought Goldhill as he paid up. He's given me two of the more expensive balloons and I don't even know if he speaks Italian with a German accent.

He shambled back to the table, defeated.

"Well," said Miriam. "Is it him?"

"How the hell would I know? He only said two words, and neither of them was Heinz or Wagner."

Miriam stared at the man again, biting her bottom lip.

"I think we should report him," said Miriam.

"Who to, that half-wit copper over there who can't even handle a bunch of hippies? And try and get the message across in Italian. Even if the policeman took

17

us seriously, we'd spend half the day down at the nick. Wouldn't be surprised if we weren't arrested ourselves in the end, the way I hear Italian police carry on," snorted Goldhill. "And if it isn't him we'll probably get done for libel or slander. All right, so it does look a bit like Wagner, but thousands of other people look like him too. If the professionals haven't been able to find him after thirty years he's never going to be found. Forget it."

Perhaps Goldhill had been too sharp with his wife, although he had always tried to understand her feelings.

She seemed to stiffen visibly. "If that's the man, he helped kill six million Jews, including my mother and father, and I think we ought to do something about it."

"Come on. The Italian police don't want to know. Don't forget they were on the same side as the Germans and a lot of the cops are still good fascists. Even if we take the trouble, nothing will happen."

"For God's sake, Sam, if those people had got to England during the war neither of us would have been sitting here now."

The pitch of Miriam's voice was rising perceptibly.

Goldhill tried to divert her. "I'm sure we'd be wasting our time with the Italian police—and I thought we were going to the Forum this afternoon."

"Forum, Shmorum. I'm going to do something about it," said Miriam, as animated as Goldhill had ever seen her, and speaking so loudly now as to attract glances from other tables.

At that moment the balloon man started hauling together his gear and making for the side street leading off the square through which he arrived and left every day, the via Sant'Agnese in Agone beside the church.

Even Goldhill was prepared to admit that the man seemed to glance in their direction as he shuffled off.

"You fool," hissed Miriam, furious now. "You were

18

talking too loud. He must have heard us and now he's running away. Quick, we must follow him."

Miriam was on her feet and calling for the waiter.

"Now listen . . ."

"Don't argue. I'm sure it's him."

The waiter came over and scrawled out one of those illegible Italian bills. Goldhill only had a ten thousand lire note, and of course the waiter had no change. He disappeared inside to the cash desk as Miriam yelled *"Subito, subito,"* one of three Italian words she knew and which was calculated to slow any Italian down to half speed, especially an Italian waiter, who would never be in a hurry to give change.

Miriam almost ran the fifty yards to the corner where the balloon man had disappeared. Goldhill handed his two balloons to a stunned but delighted child passing with his parents, and walked in after the waiter to pick up the change direct from the girl cashier. By the time he had grabbed it and walked outside, Miriam had disappeared.

He walked down to the corner and a hundred yards along to where the narrow side street was crossed by another street, the via Santa Maria dell'Anima. Miriam was standing fuming at the intersection.

"He could have gone any one of three ways," she said hopelessly, and suddenly burst into tears. Goldhill put his arm around her shoulders and tried to soothe her, but she was not to be comforted. Weeping bitterly, she said, "No one seems to care, not even you, Sam, and you're a Jew. There must be somebody somewhere . . ."

Her voice trailed off and she stopped crying. Then she said very quietly, "I'm going to tell the Israelis about this."

She turned and walked back to the Hotel Raphael a hundred yards behind the Piazza Navona as if Goldhill had ceased to exist. He looked after her, wondering what to do, and finally decided to follow her.

She nearly knocked him over at the front door, rushing out with a scrap of paper clasped in her hand.

"Where are you going?"

She waved the paper at him. "The Israeli Embassy."

"Well er—do you mind if I come, too?" asked Goldhill.

Miriam looked at him gratefully. Having made a decision, she was now nervous about it.

"I'd like it if you would, Sam," she said.

They sat silent in the taxi after showing the driver the paper with the Israeli Embassy's address copied by the hotel receptionist out of the telephone directory.

Outside the Israeli Embassy, up in the modern Parioli quarter where many diplomats lived, a gray-green uniformed Italian policeman with an ugly-looking machine-pistol bent down and peered in as the taxi drew up.

Goldhill helped Miriam out of the cab and told the guard, "We want to see someone in there."

The policeman said, "*E chiuso*," and Goldhill knew enough to understand that the Embassy was closed.

On the other side of the road he could see two field-green armored jeeps with the men in them looking out interestedly. The Embassy gate in the shrub-lined street was high, with spikes on the top, and there was a bell with a loudspeaker on the grille. Another policeman with a submachine gun was inside the gate.

"*Urgente, urgente*" said Miriam, and surprisingly the guard pointed at the bell-push and said, "*Prego*."

Goldhill pushed the buzzer, and a few seconds later a metallic voice crackled, "*Si?*"

The two policemen watched closely as Goldhill blurted, "I am sorry, I don't speak Italian, but we have some information for you."

A pause, and then the metallic voice said again, "The Embassy is closed until tomorrow morning at eight o'clock. Please return then."

Now Miriam leaned towards the microphone. "But we are flying to Paris in the morning. It will be too late then."

They heard some muttering in the background in Hebrew, and then the voice said, "Wait a minute, please."

From the watch-house beyond the gate a dark, handsome young man strolled down to the gate, looked at the couple and decided to open it. He beckoned them into the gatehouse and smiled, as the policeman inside the grounds followed them in. "I hope you don't mind," he said. "Just routine."

He ran his hands up and down Goldhill's body, tapping his pockets and feeling round the top of his socks.

"The lady's handbag, please—may I see inside?" He was turning over the contents of her large leather bag before anyone had time to answer.

It was all over in about fifteen seconds.

"Now," said the guard, as he signalled for the policeman to leave. "What is this information?"

Goldhill said simply, "We have just seen a man who closely resembles Heinz Wagner—we thought you would want to know about it."

The guard's expression did not change. They couldn't tell if he had ever heard of Wagner.

He led them towards the main building where a second guard opened a spy-hole before admitting them into the hallway.

Then the Goldhills were shown into a bare room with four chairs in it, one of them behind a desk which was bare except for an ashtray.

They sat in front of the desk, and Goldhill pulled out a cigarette. "We're wasting their time," he said. "You saw that frisking we got. They've only got time to think about the Arabs these days, not crazy tourists who claim they've seen a Nazi war criminal."

"Well, I'll feel better if we tell someone," mumbled Miriam, still upset by the personal search, as she had been on the flight to Israel at the beginning of their holiday.

Goldhill puffed at his cigarette. He had an uneasy feeling they were being watched. But only the bare white walls stared back at him.

A minute later the door opened and a tall, elegant man in shirtsleeves walked in, gray hair combed neatly back across his suntanned scalp, a writing pad and ballpoint pen in his left hand as he stretched out his right.

"Good afternoon," he said in English that was so impeccable that his slight accent was difficult to identify. "I'm Yehuda Katz, First Secretary. Sorry to keep you waiting. I understand you think you've seen someone we might be interested in."

He sat down behind the desk, looked absentmindedly in a couple of drawers and hauled out a piece of carbon paper, shoved it under the top sheet of his pad and asked, pen poised, "Would you mind giving me your names?"

Goldhill was hesitant, but Miriam, delighted at last to see someone who seemed interested, started prattling away like a machine gun. She gave their names, address, telephone number, even ages and why they were in Rome. Goldhill noted that Katz, whose real name was Yossi Bentor, was scribbling in English. Somehow he thought he might have written in Hebrew.

Miriam became quieter as she explained her background and her reasons for wanting to find Wagner. Then she described the man they had seen on the square.

It took about fifteen minutes, with Bentor writing patiently.

22

Then he put his pen down and sat back in his chair.

"It's very kind of you people to come all this way to tell me this. Naturally, you understand, the Embassy is not directly concerned in these matters. We are only concerned with representing Israel's diplomatic interests in Italy and would not dream of infringing on this country's national sovereignty. Any information of this kind we pass on to the Italian police, and it is up to them to take action. I think I should add that from my own experience in—let me see—four other embassies in which I have served, we do have a tremendous number of people coming to see us to tell us they have seen the spitting image of Bormann or Mengele or Mueller, or whoever. Much as we would like it, I'm afraid these bits of information never work out. But again, I must sincerely thank you for your trouble. I may add that if what you have said produces any positive result, we shall get word to you at the address you have given me. That would only be courteous and"—a brief smile—"sometimes there are rewards, in cases where information proves positive."

Goldhill sat bolt upright in his chair. "Look, Mr. Katz, we are not bounty seekers. I personally didn't want to come here at all. I tried to persuade my wife not to waste time on this, but after all, you must understand her feelings after what the Nazis did to her and her family. We are on holiday, and we just want to get back to sightseeing."

"Of course, of course, Mr. Goldhill," said Bentor soothingly. "I was merely trying to point out that if you hear from us, it will mean that what you have told me here has proved of some interest. If you don't hear, then of course there was nothing to it—no news, so to speak, will be bad news. As I say, we get so many of these reports that if we got in touch with all the informants we would have time for nothing else. Now, please, let me have a taxi called for you. Where would you like to go?"

He stood up and ushered them out of the room, telling the security guard at the door to call a cab.

Then he went back behind the desk, opened the drawer and switched off the tape recorder, took it upstairs to his own office and told his secretary Zipporah to transcribe the tape.

As he thumbed through the index for the 'Wagner' file, Zipporah, a stunning blonde, asked, "Do you want me to finish this tonight, darling, or can it wait till tomorrow?"

Bentor turned from the filing cabinet and said, "Zipporah, you mustn't call me 'darling' in the office."

Zipporah crossed her sensational legs and asked archly, "So where else? When I'm having dinner with you and your wife, maybe?"

Bentor sighed and turned back to the file. Zipporah had top security clearance and was supposed to be discreet. With discretion like hers, who needed a blabbermouth?

He flipped through the Wagner file. Wagner had been "seen" throughout the world, mostly in South America, two hundred and eighty three times since the war, but never in Italy. All the sightings had proved negative.

He turned and ran his hand gently through Zipporah's hair.

"Zipporah *darling*, let's have some dinner together tonight, and coffee on the Piazza Navona. When your lily white fingers have finished transcribing that tape, you'll see why."

Zipporah smiled and started pounding away at her typewriter.

Bentor wondered idly if those two English tourists would forget the whole thing. He hoped that what he had said would make them too embarrassed to talk about the incident when they got home.

Chapter Two

Just one month before Goldhill and his wife drove silently and thoughtfully away from the Israeli Embassy in Rome, a black-bearded man, six feet four inches tall and with shoulders as wide as a truck, eased himself into a wickerwork chair at a table on a cafe terrace on the Avenue des Champs Elysees. The iron-legged marble-topped table was nearest the wall, giving him a good view of anyone wending their way through the tables or passing by on the main pavement. At this time of year, there were plenty of people passing.

Blackbeard glanced over to a Citroen hovering at the curb twenty-five yards from him, in which three men were sitting, and then ordered a beer.

In that sun—and with Blackbeard's beer-drinking capacity—the beer disappeared in two long gulps. From inside the cafe a dark man in a navy blazer and gray slacks walked round to Blackbeard, whose eyes lit up in recognition.

The big man heaved himself to his feet and held out a massive hand. "Hello, Abdel, what'll you have to drink?" he asked in Arabic.

Abdel's answer was not quite what Blackbeard had in mind.

His hand came out of his blazer pocket holding a stubby .38 revolver, which he fired at Blackbeard from a range of four feet.

The first shot hit the big man in the thigh, but even before the Arab pulled the trigger, Blackbeard was reacting with stunning speed for a man his size. He grunted loudly as the bullet hit him, but his giant hands had already grabbed the underside of the heavy marble table. A weaker man would have had trouble lifting it, but Blackbeard had it up in front of him in a fraction of a second.

The Arab blasted away five more times but the bullets all smashed into the marble, gouging out pits of stone and buzzing off like enraged hornets. The six-shot revolver stopped firing, although the Arab pulled the trigger twice more. When he saw his target was still standing he cursed and flung the useless weapon at him.

In the pandemonium around the two men, customers and waiters were diving for cover or rushing back into the cafe. Blackbeard grasped the iron legs of the table and rushed the Arab, using the table top as a battering ram. If he had connected, the Arab would have been flattened. But the first bullet in the thigh had badly lamed the giant and he staggered to one side, the table crashing to the ground and shattering.

The Arab turned and ran to the curbside where a Peugeot had drawn up. A driver was sitting in it, gunning the engine, and another man was holding the two nearside doors open and shouting in Arabic.

From the Citroen, which had been waiting for Blackbeard, a short ginger-haired man who had been sitting in the front passenger seat sprinted up to the Peugeot. Police said later that what he held in his hand must have been a .22 loaded with disintegrating bullets, the kind that Israeli sky marshals favored because they devastated whatever they hit, but did not go on to hit passengers in a skyjacking.

It had a silencer, too, because later no witnesses

could recall hearing four sounds like champagne corks popping. The man holding the doors of the Peugeot collapsed, his head on the front seat, his feet still on the pavement. The Arab gunman Abdel was shot in the chest and head as he literally ran onto the Israeli's gun, and was dead before he hit the ground.

The redheaded Israeli darted over to Blackbeard, who was hopping towards the Citroen clutching his thigh, from which great spurts of blood were gushing from an arterial wound. He pushed him into the back seat where the third man was already whipping his tie off as a tourniquet.

The driver of the Arab gunman's Peugeot decided it was time to leave and his tires left black smoking tracks as he roared off with both near side doors still open. The dead man lying half across the front seat was dragged off too for a few yards, his legs kicking and bouncing off the ground crazily until he fell out when the Peugeot made a sharp right turn.

The redheaded Israeli glanced into the back seat as he jumped in beside the driver of the Citroen and one look at the blood and Blackbeard's ashen face made up his mind. "To hell with their driver," he snapped. "We need a doctor quickly."

Blackbeard mumbled, "Some informer Abdel turned out to be! Remind me to cross him off my lunch list," before he passed out.

Fifteen minutes later a telephone rang in a flat beyond the Arc de Triomphe out in Neuilly. The woman who answered it heard the ginger-haired gunman say, "Get a doctor over to us fast. The bleeding's stopped but that could be either because the tourniquet's working or the poor bastard's just run out of blood."

Mary Steiger could not at first identify the noise as she was roused from a deep sleep in her apartment at Bat Yam south of Tel Aviv. Then she realized someone was hammering insistently at the door. She turned in the double bed and then remembered David would not be there. Off on one of his frequent and mysterious business trips.

She looked at her watch—two o'clock in the morning —as she pulled on a dressing gown.

Through the peephole in the front door she saw a young woman and a man.

"What is it?" she said through the door.

The young woman said, "Your husband has had an accident, but he is not going to die. Will you come with us, please?"

Her heart pounded as she flung on some clothes and drove in fearful silence north through Tel Aviv and out east of the city to Tel Hashomer hospital. Her usually massive, bearded husband looked surprisingly small and white as he lay back in the hospital bed with a drip-feed attached to his arm. He opened his eyes and smiled weakly as she walked over to him.

"Sorry, love," said Steiger. "I got into a bit of a scrape and lost a lot of blood, so they tell me. But the Doc says I'll be up and about again in a while."

Mary had heard reports of the Paris shooting on the Israeli radio, and the description of the black-bearded man who was wounded.

She clasped her husband's gigantic hand in both hers and asked quietly, "Where did you get hurt, Dave?"

Steiger pulled back the bedclothes and showed a mass of bandages on his right thigh.

Mary started sobbing uncontrollably.

"Dave," she said, "you know I never ask you about your work, and I'm not asking you now. But it all seems downright dangerous, and in Johannesburg you were doing so well in real estate before we came to Israel."

Steiger patted his wife's cheek and smiled at the thought of the name plate on the office door in Tel Aviv which his wife had never seen.

It said: "Viktor Halsmann Co., Real Estate Agents."

"No sweat," he said gently. "It's nothing. I just cut myself shaving."

Chapter Three

When the hamseen, the hot desert wind from the Sinai and Negev deserts, blows into Tel Aviv in July, the heat is unbearable. The sun seems to be watery but it beats down relentlessly on the streets and the roof-tops of what is basically an ugly city, built in haste to accommodate the influx of Jews from all over the world. For most of the immigrants the hastily built box-shaped houses were like a corner in Paradise after the holocaust in Europe in which six million of them had died.

Never again, thought the immigrants as they kissed the soil of Israel, would there be the pogroms, the mid-night knock, the cattle trains packed with Jews destined for the extermination camps. Here they were home, in a land peopled by Jews, run by Jews, for Jews.

But the temporary houses had become permanent in this city and many of the walls were peeling. Space in the few solid old houses or the new apartment blocks was at a premium. And few of them had air condition-ing, an essential in the Middle East. Half of every pound the Israelis paid in tax went in defense costs—and they were now paying higher taxes than any other nation in the world.

The Israelis grumbled, but they knew they were get-ting their money's worth. Four times, in 1948, 1956,

1967 and 1973, the New Jews had warded off another holocaust. This time the oppressors were not the German Master Race, the men in coal-scuttle helmets with jack-booted officers who worked their way methodically through the terrified ghettos of Europe. This time the oppressors were the Arabs surrounding the new state, fifty million of them around Israel's borders, who considered Palestine had been stolen from them, compressing the two and a half million Israelis into a giant ghetto.

But this was a ghetto with a difference.

The native-born Israelis, the Sabras, sometimes referred contemptuously to the European immigrants as "soaps," despising them for allowing themselves to be destroyed piecemeal by the Germans, destroyed so completely that the gold extracted from their teeth after their last naked walk into the gas chambers was salted away by the Nazis in such quantities that it supplied the hunted Germans who fled after the war with fortunes for their exile. And from the rest of the corpses the Germans experimented, making lampshades with human skins, and bars of soap.

The Ghetto of Israel had a carapace like an armadillo. The nation's young men and women were lean and fit. They formed one of the best small fighting forces the world had ever seen. Some of the houses might be shabby, but the Armed Forces had everything they needed. Things were getting tougher all the time. The arrogance of the Israelis after their stunning victory in the Six Day War in 1967 had been replaced by the gloom and anxiety created by the near-debacle at the beginning of the Yom Kippur War in 1973.

After the Six Day War the deputy mayor of Tel Aviv had joked, "Israel is a peace-loving nation. We've got a piece of Egypt, a piece of Jordan and a piece of Syria— and we love it."

32

There were no jokes during and after the Yom Kippur War. The Arabs had smartened up and the Israelis had grown careless, believing in the myth of their own invincibility after the Egyptian and Jordanian Air Forces were destroyed on the ground in the first hundred and seventy minutes of the Six Day War. In that war the Israeli Air Force reckoned to "turn a plane round" when it came back to base after a strafing mission in just four minutes. The Egyptian President of the day, Gamal Abdel Nasser, was convinced he was being attacked by British and American war planes as well, since there were so many Israeli pilots airborne at the same time. That, in any case, was what he told King Hussein of Jordan in a telephone call neatly intercepted by Israeli wiretappers.

On the ground, Israeli Centurions, Pattons and Shermans had sliced through the Egyptian, Jordanian and Syrian Armored Corps like a knife through butter in 1967.

Until then the cornerstone of Israel's military policy was that no Arab nation could ever be allowed to choose the moment of attack. If the Israeli Ghetto was to survive it had to carry the war into the enemy's lands. It had to have that perfect sense of timing to know just when and where the Arabs were mustering their might—and where the first Israeli hammer blow would, in effect, be the last in any major conflict.

To help in the timing Israel had a Military Intelligence Bureau and a Secret Service which were the envy of their rivals from the KGB to the CIA.

But even crack secret services can make mistakes, and they made a horrific one before the Yom Kippur War. They knew the Syrian and Egyptian armies were massing, but assumed it was another bluff or maneuver of the kind they had detected several times before.

Israel was caught with badly lowered dungarees by the new Egyptian soldier-president Anwar Sadat, who was able to storm across the Suez Canal and prove that the Israelis could be beaten—at least for a few days.

Israeli planes were knocked out of the sky by the Arabs' sophisticated Soviet rockets. Her tanks were decimated and she just managed to stop Syrian tanks short of Israel proper as they thundered across the Golan Heights. Israel's brilliant armored counterattack across the Suez Canal led by General Ariel Sharon left her in a winning position when the guns stopped firing but more than two and a half thousand of her best fighting men had been killed.

And in the political aftermath she had been forced to hand back more land on the Egyptian and Syrian fronts, as the powerful Arab oil lobby put the pressure on everywhere. Top politicians and generals were sacked for the blunder, and Israel was now desperately trying to produce her own fighters, gunboats, missiles— even a rifle with a bottleopener on it—against the day when the Arab armies felt strong enough for a final assault.

Press reports stated that Israel could also put together nuclear bombs just in case everything else failed —because everyone in Israel knew what failure would mean.

In the meantime, the perpetual intelligence work went on, in the hopes of there being no more critical mistakes.

In a four-floor apartment block in Tel Aviv's Gordon Street on this particular July day, David Steiger, with a temporary desk job while he recovered from his injuries in the Paris shooting, was melting under a slowly turning fan and wondering when the Department would get around to approving air conditioning for the building. "Any day now," they had been saying for four years.

Steiger, a South African who still spoke Hebrew with an atrocious accent, felt the heat badly. Here he was, acting head of the section, gulping soft drinks by the gallon and sweating them out almost instantaneously, and across the hallway were a bunch of junior cipher clerks relaxing in the building's one air conditioned room.

It had to be air conditioned because of the machinery in it.

During the hamseen Steiger would often wander into the cipher room just to cool off. At first glance it looked just about the same as any newspaper's wire room, packed with teleprinter machines. But these teleprinters were different. Instead of the massive newspaper teleprinters which hammered the words like giant typewriters onto carbon rolls, these machines were small, about the size of a portable typewriter. And although they had keyboards, the machines did not clatter as they received or sent messages. There was just an odd electric buzz as if a loose wire was sparking every time it made a contact. The words were appearing on the paper as if by magic as the sparking noise spat from a small nozzle riding along a well-oiled bar in front of the paper. A close look at the printed letters showed they had been formed by a series of tiny dots.

In one corner of the windowless room stood a large steel box bulging with hundreds of tiny transistorized circuit cards and a panel with winking red, green and yellow tell-tale lights. One or several of the lights flickered every time a spark emerged from one of the "teleprinters" ranged along the other side of the room.

The idea was that coded messages coming in from abroad had a frequently changed prefix which triggered the decoding mechanism of the computer. This unscrambled the messages and sent them in clear to the teleprinter. In the more expensively appointed stations

35

abroad there was similar electronic machinery so that an agent sending a message to Tel Aviv could type in clear provided he put the correct prefix on the message. The computers at each end scrambled and unscrambled the text. It was an expensive way of doing away with code books, but it saved time, and there were no code books lying around for prying eyes. All the sending agent had to remember was the prefix, and this he carried around in his head.

If an agent anywhere in the world was arrested, or simply disappeared, the prefix was instantly changed.

The computer handled other things too. It could send and receive "scrambled" photographs. These were sent in the same way as newspapermen send radio or wire pictures around the world, on a receiving and sending drum. But anyone tapping an ordinary telephoto frequency could "lift" the picture. The computer the Department supplied ensured scrambling during transmission into an incomprehensible black-and-white jigsaw.

Steiger stood idly in the room, a cigarette in one hand and a Coca-Cola bottle almost entirely concealed in one massive fist, as he cooled off and stared at the white overalled backs of his three clerks.

One of the clerks tore a message off one teleprinter and turned.

"Oh, sorry. I didn't realize you were here. This one's for you from Rome."

Steiger took the message and walked slowly back into the steamy afternoon heat of his office. Rome was having trouble these days from the Palestinians. The Embassy staff knew they were being followed. At least one planned attack on the Embassy by four Arabs had failed, but they kept trying. Embassy staffs everywhere in the world had to go about in pairs, clock in and clock out, take irregular routes from the Embassies to their homes, and call on arrival at every point. The phone bills were going up as a thousand diplomats and their families in a hundred countries kept the lines humming.

You couldn't always win. The Arabs had captured the Embassy in Bangkok a couple of years ago and held several staff members at gunpoint as they demanded the release of terrorists jailed in Israel. The kidnappers had finally been talked into flying to Cairo without their hostages by the Thai army and the local Egyptian Ambassador. The Egyptians had at least realized that something unpleasant could happen to one of their Embassies if Israelis got into serious trouble abroad.

Lately the Arab Black September gang had been giving big trouble. They didn't care if an Arab Embassy got blown up. As exiled Palestinians who thought the land the Israelis were sitting on rightly belonged to them, they had nothing to lose. Apart from Steiger's own near shave in Paris, a couple of good Israeli agents and three diplomats had been gunned down or blown up by letter bombs.

One or two Arabs had been found dead, too.

But it wasn't good enough, thought Steiger. It was no good going around blasting Arab agents when the ratio of Arabs to Jews around Israel's borders was twenty to one. And Steiger was also bound by a political directive. Israeli counter measures against Arab terrorists were not to degenerate into shootouts between Arab and Jewish gunmen on the streets of Europe. Israel had to appear to follow the rules of law and order in the host countries.

Steiger clenched his mighty fist on the Coke bottle as he thought about the political directive, almost powdering the glass. "Goddam politicians," he muttered. "If I had my way there wouldn't be an Arab Embassy standing anywhere in Europe today. Those bloody wogs would soon put the squeeze on the Black September mob then."

He thought back to the good old days, when a few of the lads had blown the British Embassy in Rome sky high during the Palestine troubles, and a few more had swiped Eichmann from under the nose of the Argentinos and flown him back to the hangman in Israel.

"Goddam politicians," Steiger snarled again. Everyone, with the possible exception of the British, had thought the Embassy job was a very neat piece of work. And the Eichmann coup was the envy of all the other Secret Services. None of today's namby-pamby diplomatic niceties then, he thought, as he brushed the flies off his desk and put down the message from Rome.

It read: "*Section X Department BL. from Sub-Section ADX* Serial 22845/4. Originator Bentor. Attention Steiger. SUBJECT: WAGNER Heinz.

"Acting on information received from British tourists Samuel Goldhill and his wife Miriam of 40-42 John II Street, London WC8N 3DC I have checked the appearance of balloon hawker at Piazza Navona, described by informants as being similar to Colonel Heinz Wagner on Nuremburg List. Accompanying me was clerk Zipporah Harel. Allowing for age difference of some thirty years we both found similarity striking particularly regarding hairline, ears, gray eyes, height approximately six feet. His Italian is good but with marked accent which could be German. Habitués and restaurant staff on square only know he has been around several years, as long as some of the young waiters can remember. He appears to have no friends and never talks to anyone on the square. He does not frequent any of the many cafes on the square. Suspect also presumably lives nearby as hydrogen cylinder he brings to square to inflate balloons looks fairly heavy and he always disappears and emerges from same street. He also carries light trestle table and fold-over leather pouch. In the one week we have been observing him he sets up trestle on which he places balloons and puts pouch on ground between trestle and right foot. We have never seen him open pouch. Money he takes for balloons and change he gives all come out of trouser pockets. He is doing quite good business at this time of the year, selling about forty balloons a day. Estimated profit after providing gas and strings for balloons— about six thousand five hundred lire a day, which means he's not dining out every night. Have not attempted to follow or attract attention by making any further inquiries. Await your instructions. Shalom. Ends message."

Steiger read the message through twice. Bentor was a good man, one of the best from the old days and an ex-concentration camp inmate. Not a man to say more than he believed. Not a man to bother him with unnecessary decisions in the middle of the anti-terrorist campaign.

He sent down for the Wagner file. It was pretty dusty. After his "grave" was discovered by the CIA in 1947 nobody had been looking for him particularly. Then, in 1963, a Nazi-hunting agency based in Europe said they were hearing reports that Wagner was alive, possibly in Austria. After some pressure the Germans were persuaded to exhume the bones in the Berlin suburban grave and found the remains of three people, one of them probably a woman, neither of the other two Wagner. A local newspaperman had got hold of the story and it was a two-day sensation. After that people were seeing Wagners all over the place—in South America, Vienna, Eastern Europe, you name it. Checking out was difficult. There were no known fingerprints or dental charts. Wagner's dentist was dead. He had had eighteen clear years to cover his tracks.

Wagner's son and daughter said the coffin they believed contained their father's body had been delivered to them one night by a group of Germans who said they were "ex-colleagues" and couldn't give their names. They said they only knew he had been killed in the Berlin debacle in May 1945, probably by Russian gunfire. Someone was taking the trouble to cover up for Wagner—and there were still plenty of Nazis about in those days. Whose bodies were in the coffin? Who knew? Bodies were two a penny at the end of the war. Wagner's "widow" was living in Munich. The colour of his eyes was given as gray, height six feet and one-half inch. And there were some more details. No one had even claimed seeing Wagner in the past three years.

Except the Goldhills, Bentor and the girl clerk.

Steiger decided to invest a little more time on the sighting. To his secretary he dictated a cable to Bentor: "Probentor exsteiger your 22845 oblique four methinks worth getting usual contact take usual pix particularly skull all angles comma ears comma nose comma full front and side stop wire best ten soonest stop take no rpt no other action until advised steiger."

It was late. Steiger looked in on the duty officer on his way downstairs and said, "I'm going along to the Tar Bar for a couple on the way home. If my wife calls, tell her I'll be home in about an hour."

Steiger on the move looked like an attacking Centurion tank. He was six feet four from the floor up and nearly as wide from side to side. In his youth he had looked like a Greek god. Now he looked more like a goddam Greek. He had a tendency to turn slightly sideways when he walked through doors, after years of hitting doorjambs. The door frames got a worse deal out of it than Steiger's shoulders whenever he connected. The staircase creaked ominously as he lumbered down it surprisingly fast, despite a slight limp still persisting from the Paris wound.

On the ground floor he peeked through a small one-way mirror in a door leading to the ground floor offices and hit a buzzer. The door swung open and Steiger walked through two office rooms where secretaries were busily typing.

"How's business?" he called to a sallow-faced shirt-sleeved man in the inner office.

"Not bad," said the man. "We actually sold three houses today. If it goes on like this we can forget your bit upstairs."

Steiger walked through the front door past a man at the reception desk and slammed it behind him, rattling the loose Real Estate Agents' nameplate.

He shambled, head down, three blocks west towards the seafront, turned right on Dizengoff Street and pushed a swing door open into the Tar Bar. Until he left the office he rarely drank, even at lunchtime.

But in the evenings his massive frame needed infusions of industrial quantities of Scotch and soda, which had no noticeable effect. He had read somewhere that Scotch was good for the heart, and he planned to prove it even if it killed him. On this particular evening the Tar Bar was quiet. The usual live pop group was missing and in their place was a violinist, a cellist and a pianist playing a tired selection from Franz Lehar. The average age of the group was nine hundred and three. The only thing missing to put the whole atmosphere back into the nineteen-twenties was a Palm Court.

As Steiger walked in, a tourist was asking the violinist despairingly, "Well, can you play *South Pacific*, at least?"

The violinist leaned over to him from the bandstand and said in a thick Russian accent, "Listen, this is a three-piece orchestra, and *South Pacific* isn't one of them."

41

Steiger nodded to the regular bar tart slumped over her drink and she nodded back. She knew better than to bother him, even if the place was nearly deserted.

The barman poured a slug of Scotch from Steiger's regular bottle that would have felled an ox as Eli, the owner, came over to say hello. Eli winced slightly as Steiger crushed his fingers in a Herculean grip and said, "It's quiet tonight. I just don't know where everyone's got to."

Steiger and Eli both knew. They had both fought against the Arab armies in 1948 down in the Gaza Strip. Eli was a Rumanian, Steiger a South African, but they had plenty in common from those days. Eli and Steiger were the only survivors of their infantry platoon. And Eli knew that Steiger wasn't just a real estate man. But he never asked questons.

Eli did, however, know that his pop group, all young Armored Corps men, had suddenly disappeared—as they often did. And he knew that a lot of other young regulars were not in the bar tonight. He also knew that a bazooka shell fired over the Golan Heights from the Syrian lines two days earlier had killed an Israeli soldier.

Eli just didn't know exactly when and where the reprisal was planned.

Steiger knew it was at four o'clock the next morning and that his twenty-four year old son would be in the first tanks to attack. He signalled for another Scotch, because he planned to be fairly bow-legged by the time he got home. He couldn't tell his wife, so he might as well delay going home anyway.

Chapter Four

Steiger got to his home in Bat Yam south of Tel Aviv at about midnight. His wife Mary, a surprisingly slight woman to be married to such a human mountain, asked no questions. She had long ago learned that whatever her husband was doing he couldn't tell her about it. She had a number to call for him at the office, but didn't know where it was except that it was somewhere in Tel Aviv. When she checked the number earlier in the evening a man's voice had just said, "He should have been home by now, but maybe he got delayed. Nothing to worry about."

Now as Mary looked at him as he came home from the Tar Bar, Steiger realized ironically that there was a look of relief on her face. She could always tell when he'd been giving a Scotch bottle a really hard time, which was more than most of his colleagues could do, but she must have been one of the few women in the world who would realize that he sometimes had to unwind.

"Did you eat?" she asked.

"Yes, thanks," said Steiger. "I had a couple of oink sandwiches on the way home. I think I'll turn in, as I've got a big day tomorrow."

"Oink" is the Israeli euphemism for ham.

Steiger lay staring up at the ceiling as Mary slept

43

quietly beside him, enveloped in his tree trunk of a left arm. He must have dozed off for a while, but then he suddenly woke up. He looked at the luminous hands of his watch.

It was four o'clock. The men, including his son Joe, would just be finishing their final briefing now in the headlights of the assembled half-tracks and tanks. In a few minutes the old half-tracks, a job-lot war surplus purchase from the Americans which had been miraculously kept going for quarter of a century longer than intended, would be loading up with men and ammunition, each with a heavy machine gun at the front and two side-mounted .303 Brownings. There would be a few of the newer M.113 armored personnel carriers. And the tanks, quietly trundled up in transporters during the night to their assembly points, would kick their massive engines into life.

Joe Steiger was a tank commander. His father knew that the commanders always fought with their heads and shoulders sticking out of the top of the turret hatches. It gave quicker all-round vision—but in the Yom Kippur War the Israelis had lost a lot of tank commanders.

Steiger slipped quietly out of bed, brewed himself some Turkish coffee and walked out onto their small balcony overlooking the Mediterranean. The Hamseen still made the pre-dawn night oppressive, and Steiger knew the insides of the tanks would be like ovens later in the day.

Steiger hoped his wife would have slept through the seven o'clock news. Most people in Israel had built-in alarm clocks and lived on their transistors, every hour on the hour.

But she was coming out of the bedroom as he walked over to switch on the radio.

The Kol Yisrael (Voice of Israel) newsreader said,

"At dawn today an armored group and motorized infantry of the Israeli Defense Forces entered Lebanon from the northeast corner of Israel. The task force is on a search and destroy mission seeking groups of terrorists occupying the area. Shortly after the attack began, Syrian artillery opened fire across the Golan Heights. The fire is being returned. At six o'clock Israeli Air Force planes struck in support of the task force in the Lebanon and several other strikes were made against Syrian artillery and tank positions. Two Syrian artillery positions were silenced and one Syrian tank was knocked out. The operation is continuing."

Mary looked at her husband. "Is he—is Joe—?"

"I think he may be," said Steiger.

He bathed, shaved and dressed quickly.

"I'll call you if there's anything," he said as he kissed his wife goodbye.

Israel never announced the death of a soldier before his relatives had been told. That way, if the radio said a man had been killed, anyone listening knew it could not be their son, brother or husband.

By the time Steiger reached his office there was precious little work going on. The cipher clerks had their ears glued to the radio and the secretaries were crowded round them.

"Let's hope the boys are knocking the hell out of them," said one of the cipher clerks.

A pregnant secretary whose husband of six months was in the Armored Corps stared blankly at her typewriter keys.

By eleven o'clock it was all over. All the Israeli armor had pulled back inside the Israeli border. Steiger went one floor down into another office. The man there said, "Two of our boys were killed and one seriously wounded." He handed Steiger a typewritten list.

Steiger read the names and walked back upstairs.

To the pregnant secretary he said, as he dialed his wife, "He's OK."

To Mary he said, "Don't worry. Joe's all right."

As he hung up the cipher clerk leaned in and said, "Pictures for you from Rome—and they're not of Sophia Loren."

Steiger told his secretary to send the Heinz Wagner picture file down to the projection room and added, "Tell the bumps man I want him there in half an hour."

He walked into the teleprinter room where the pictures of the balloon man were rolling off at the rate of one every twelve minutes, half speed for better quality. That meant the ten he had asked for would take two hours arriving. But three were in already.

Steiger grabbed them and went down to the projection room. The Wagner file was already there and Steiger made a quick comparison between the three balloon man photos he already had and the pictures on file. The balloon man was older, obviously, and thinner—but then, who wouldn't be on his kind of money. And the jug-ears looked the same in both sets.

Tibi, the "bumps" man, came in, and so did two more pictures from Rome.

For two hours Steiger and Tibi sat there as the projectionist switched on the pictures, side by side and from time to time superimposing them. "The nose is a bit fleshier on the younger man," said Tibi. "But that's normal. The older man's hairline is slightly further back, but that's normal too. The jaws match up. But get those ears—they're dead ringers. They stick out at the same angle from front and side views. For jug ears there is an unusually long lobe."

And from the best front and side views they superimposed exactly.

Tibi looked at Steiger. "For my money, there's a

ninety-five percent chance they're the same guy."

Within half an hour Steiger was in the Department Chief's office with the pictures and the report from Rome.

The Chief was a small man with a shock of still-black hair graying at the temples and a pair of large horn-rimmed glasses. People did not notice him in the street. He had given up four packs of cigarettes a day to cure his cough and had recently taken to cigars that smelt like something left in the desert for a few decades by Lawrence's Camel Corps. He still had a cough.

"Let's not go hog wild about this," he said after examining Steiger's exhibits. "In the first place, try and find out his name and where he lives. Don't tell the Italian police about it yet."

As Steiger was leaving he added, "No harm in getting a set of his dabs and finding out what's in that pouch he carries all the time."

Chapter Five

Peter Keane, a tall, slender young Second Secretary at the British Embassy in Rome, told the taxi driver to let him off at the corner of Passetto's Restaurant just off the Piazza Navona. On these warm summer evenings he liked to walk through the Piazza to his new home on the via di Parione, three blocks behind the square, and perhaps stop for a drink at the Tre Scalini giving a good view of the square—and, just as important for bachelor Keane, a good view of the passing girls. The Piazza Navona was rather like the Champs Elysees in Paris. If you sat there long enough, someone you knew was bound to pass by.

Keane had recently discovered Campari and soda, something that at first tasted like pink mouthwash but became addictive. Must be the quinine in it, thought Keane as he sipped gently at his first.

On the square itself the evening performance was about to begin. Young students, hippies and some of the Eternal City's artist colony had begun to arrive and set up their stands. The hippies spread blankets out on the ground and arranged their offerings of wire jewelry. Students handed out leaflets advocating everything from violent overthrow of the Government to abortion-for-all. Some of the artists were pretty good, and so were their prices.

City police patrolmen looked on all these activities fairly benevolently, even on the students. Plotting the violent overthrow of the Government was largely an academic exercise. By the time plans were set, the Government of the day would have collapsed anyway, unless you moved with lightning speed. Italy, reflected Keane, was a miracle country which seemed to stagger on, running itself despite its nearly forty post-Mussolini premiers.

Keane saw that the balloon man he had noticed several times before on the square had a new line in addition to his balloons. He was selling brightly colored birds with flapping wings and an elastic wind-up thread to make them go. In the dusk they were pretty convincing. The wings whirred like a pigeon on a fast take-off and the birds wheeled and turned in an eccentric pattern across the square until the elastic unwound and they glided to the ground. The children were going wild for them. The balloon man was doing a roaring trade.

Then it all turned into an Italian farce.

An Italian father had just bought his child one of the birds. The child wound the elastic and immediately hurled it into the air. It was a bad launch. The bird shot straight along about two feet from the ground, turned and zoomed back in at the startled child, whistled over the top of the balloon man's head and dived in for a second run. A young man stood nearby with his arm round a girl and an enormous Great Dane on a short leash, looking at an artist's painting. The bird, wings whistling, fluttered up behind the unsuspecting dog. The Great Dane turned and in a reflex action bounded from his master's hand and with one giant gulp grabbed the bird between its jaws. As the bird still flapped frantically the Great Dane lowered it to the ground and walloped a massive paw on the fluttering wings, trying to figure out what was happening.

There was an instant wail from the child as it saw its new toy being torn to shreds. The couple who owned the dog burst out laughing when they saw what was happening, and the child's father started yelling at them to call their hound off. Keane even saw an elderly English tourist couple, thinking it was a real pigeon, start jabbing at the dog with a walking stick with cries of "disgraceful." The dog let go of the bird and turned to face his new attackers, the child grabbed for its toy, the child's father started pushing the dog owner, who stopped laughing instantly and started shoving back, and there was all-around pandemonium as various people fought off the dog, the owner, the stick-waving Britons and the Italian child's family.

A patrolman started walking over as the shoving melee stumbled back and forth like a rugby scrum. In the middle of all this the balloon man was knocked flat on his back. His trestle table collapsed and his hydrogen cylinder fell with a thud and started hissing alarmingly. There were balloons, wind-up pigeons, dogs, people and escaping gas all over the place. The cop waded in, adding to the confusion, and lost his hat for his trouble. The balloon man was scrambling around frantically on the pavement trying to get his belongings together.

Keane noticed a young man trying to help the balloon man to his feet and another picking up the balloon man's black leather pouch, which had been kicked about fifteen feet away.

And Keane noticed the man who picked up the pouch open the flap quickly and peer inside as he stood wth his back to the balloon man.

Keane, who had been rolling about helpless with laughter up till then, watched the man holding the pouch carefully. But the young man did not put his hand in the pouch. He closed the flap and turned to hand it back to the balloon man.

51

My God, thought Keane, those two fellows were trying to rob him in the confusion—but obviously he doesn't keep his money in the pouch. You couldn't be too careful in Italy, especially after, Keane had read, latest statistics showed that as many cars were stolen every year in Italy as in Britain, Germany and France combined, and that someone was robbed every sixty-five seconds. The two young men were dusting down the balloon man, helping him set up his trestle and finding his birds and balloons as the confusion died down. Keane noticed that one of the men even bought a couple of balloons. The balloon man sullenly produced the change out of his pocket as he clutched the leather pouch under his arm.

Those guys only bought the balloon to find out which pocket he kept his money in, Keane thought.

But the balloon man had obviously had enough. He started gathering his gear together as Keane ordered another Campari and idly waited for the next slice of Roman life to unfold.

The two young men wandered off and seemed to lose interest in the hawker.

Keane noticed a couple at the table next to him. They had been watching the incident too. The first thing that caught his roving eye was the girl. She was really a stunner, with straw blonde hair and dark brown skin from hours in the sun, naked on a terrace somewhere, thought Keane lecherously. Her eyes were a startling ice-blue. Keane glanced casually at her companion, an older man with gray hair combed back over his head, also suntanned. How do these old guys get these girls, Keane grumbled to himself, and then realized that the man was vaguely familiar. Probably some randy old sod with pots of money who gets his picture in the society gossip columns with his latest acquisition. Keane's stare became faintly hostile as he thought about it. Then he saw that the man was looking back at him, and inclined his head slightly in a sign of recognition.

Keane, who had only arrived in Rome two months before, had met dozens of people at diplomatic cocktail parties and dinners, but hadn't been able to sort out all the names yet. He reckoned the other man was having the same trouble trying to remember where they had met. Keane nodded back and waved his hand slightly. I don't care who it is, he thought, but I wouldn't mind getting a crack at his girl.

He contemplated the idea of just lumbering over to the table and re-introducing himself, but at that point the waiter brought the couple their change and they stood up. The girl was slightly taller than the man and of statuesque proportions.

Keane could feel his temperature rise as the girl stared straight at him out of her cold eyes, and the man murmured "Good evening" in English as they sauntered by. He followed them with his eyes but they turned the corner immediately up the via Sant'Agnese in Agone, a few yards behind the balloon man who was carrying his gear off the square.

It wasn't until a few minutes later that Keane remembered the man was someone from the Israeli Embassy he had met at a cocktail party, who had been described to him as "one of their top spooks here."

Next morning in the office he flipped through the diplomatic list and recalled the name as he looked through the Israeli entry. There it was: Yehuda Katz, First Secretary and Cultural Attaché. Katz was shown as having a Mrs. Katz with him in Rome. Keane had been introduced to Katz and his wife. He didn't remember what the wife looked like—but one thing he was positive about.

She didn't look anything like the staggering blonde

53

he had been squiring on the Piazza Navona last night.

Embassies were supposed to keep an eye on each other's spooks.

Keane strolled out of his office and into the room of the man who was in charge of such things, Keane's immediate superior, and said: "Joe, what has two arms, two legs and sleeps with cats?"

Joe Burke looked puzzled.

"The answer, my friend, is Mrs. Katz and sometimes a delicious, tall, blonde bird I saw him with at the Piazza Navona last night!"

Burke groaned, but looked interested. "How do you know he's having it off and away with her, then?" he asked.

"I don't," said Keane. "But if he's not, he's stark raving bonkers. This one is . . ." His voice trailed away as his hands traced the air lasciviously.

Burke grunted, and went about his business thoughtfully. He filed the bit of scandal away in his head and put a mental red tag on it.

Chapter Six

The hamseen had cleared up and everyone was in a better mood in Tel Aviv. With the sun blinds down on the fourth floor at Gordon Street, one could just about keep the temperature bearable. Steiger had halved his iced Coke intake and was no longer dripping sweat all over the latest reports on the furtive war around the world between the Arab terrorists and the Israeli counter-terrorist commandos. The largest evening newspaper in Israel, *Maariv* was leading on a story from Paris about an Egyptian who had been found dead, his hands and feet tied, on the banks of the Seine just below the gold-statued Alexandre III bridge.

The *Maariv* reporter in Paris quoted a police spokesman as saying the Egyptian had severe head injuries and appeared to have fallen from the bridge. But the police were still investigating the possibility of a bizarre suicide, as the man's bonds were only loosely tied and his head injuries could have been inflicted by the fall.

Steiger permitted himself a humorless laugh and told the secretary who lent him the paper, "If the French cops work really hard on that one they may even conclude he shot himself in the back with a knife."

The Egyptian's death gave Steiger some personal satisfaction. For he knew the man was the Arab driver of the car who escaped during the shootout on the

Champs Elysees months before when Steiger himself was hit.

That, he thought, made it three out of three for the Israelis as he ruefully rubbed the bullet scar on his right thigh, which was still keeping him out of the field.

The cipher clerk came in and told him there were two "urgents" for him from Rome—one report and one picture.

The picture turned out to be fingerprints of the balloon man's full right hand and a thumb and forefinger print of the left hand taken off a balloon he sold to two Israeli agents the day before.

The message was a report from Bentor. It outlined the incident on the Piazza Navona which had given the Israelis a golden opportunity to move in after a week's tight surveillance following the new instructions from Tel Aviv in which there had been no chance to get a look inside the balloon man's foldover pouch.

The next part made Steiger sit up.

"Agent 224 managed to open the pouch without the suspect seeing and saw inside, among other objects which he was unable to identify as they were wrapped in newspaper, a short-barrelled Smith & Wesson .38 revolver. The revolver was loaded at least in the three chambers the agent was able to see on the side facing him. There was also a box for .38 cartridges which the agent did not have time to open to see if it was full or empty."

Bentor's report went on: "The suspect has been followed to his home, which is an attic on the fifth floor of a tenement house in the Vicolo del Fico. He buys the balloons and wind-up pigeons he sells on the square at (Bentor gave the address). He changes his hydrogen cylinder at (another address). The storekeepers at both these addresses know him as Signor Kent. The gas cylinder supplier seems to remember Kent once telling him he was Dutch, but is not sure. We have not pushed questioning of these two witnesses so far to avoid arousing undue suspicion or possibly a remark to Kent the next time he calls. He makes minor purchases of food and vegetables in the market at the Piazza del Fico, a few yards from his home. He also buys kerosene which indicates he cooks in his room on a stove and has no city gas. All his purchases are modest, well within the bounds of the likely income he makes from selling balloons. He has received no mail in the week he has been under intensive surveillance. His home is about two hundred yards from the Piazza Navona and all his purchases are made around the same area. He has had no visitors and indulges in no casual conversation with shopkeepers or market stallholders. He has not left the area during the week. He sometimes crosses the street for no apparent reason and often glances over his shoulder. He carries the pouch with the gun at all times, even when he leaves his home for a few minutes to buy a loaf of bread. This indicates to me that he is in fear of being attacked rather than planning some criminal enterprise. In my opinion it weighs very heavily in confirming our suspicions as to his true identity."

You can say that again, Yossi, thought Steiger.

He opened a file which he had started building up on the latest information about Heinz Wagner. The first document was a copy of a report received by a Deportees Association, which made it its business to keep looking for escaped Nazi war criminals, from the Berlin Public Prosecutor's office.

Der Generalstaatsanwalt bei dem Landgericht.
Ref 6 J (M) Js 47.68.
Investigation of Heinz Wagner for crimes.
Ref: your letter of 19th July.

Dear Sir,

As a result of investigations to date the following persons are in the best position to identify the accused:

1) His wife Barbara Wagner of Munich
2) His son Guenther of Krefeld-Bochum
3) His former mistresses: Anna Rueder of Munich, Sophie Bauer of Berlin
4) Ex-SS Brigadefuehrer and General of Police Josef Brandt of Munich
5) Ex-SS Obersturmfuehrer and former colleague of the accused Albert Schwarzkopf of Kiel

As regards special peculiarities of the accused we have learned the following.

Wagner was tall and powerfully built. He was a competent mountaineer. He was not wounded during the Second World War. He suffered from a stomach disorder and is reported to have preferred boiled foods. He is believed to have undergone an appendectomy in 1938.

Shape of Wagner's head

Anna Rueder: Long, oval shaped.

Brandt: Squarish skull, large back of the head, narrow aquiline nose, large mouth but usually pursed lips, gray eyes.

Guenther Wagner: Very big head, large at the back, took a large size in hats, ears sticking out from the head with long lobes, small scar visible on one eyelid when closed, gray eyes.

Sophie Bauer: Large, especially at the back, wide forehead, small sunken eyes, strong nose but narrow nostrils, strong chin, ordinary sized hats too small for him.

Schwarzkopf: Rather an "a la Hindenburg" head, strong chin, high domed forehead.

SS records: Head circumference 58 centimeters.

Barbara Wagner: Small scar on the right forehead.

Wagner's teeth

Brandt: Quite good teeth, if any dentures would only be on upper row, perhaps gold filling at back, no holes in front teeth.

Son Guenther: Good strong teeth with a smoker's yellow film, gold fillings at back.

Anna Rueder: Positive Wagner had good teeth with no dentures, regular, healthy, no special peculiarities.

Sophie Bauer: Good strong teeth but yellowed by smoking quite heavily, no dentures, false teeth or crowns. Remembers no dental treatment.

Schwarzkopf: Until he last saw him in May 1943 Wagner had no upper nor lower dentures, could not recall whether Wagner had ever been to the dentist.

Feet

Brandt: Size 45 (German)

SS Records: Size 43

Son Guenther: Possibly a surgical scar on one heel.

Hands

Brandt: Strong, athletic, was competent mountaineer.
Sophie Bauer: Short hands with wide fingers, gloves
   size 40.

Height and Shape

Brandt: 175 cms.
Sophie Bauer: about 180 cms.
Anna Rueder: between 178-180 cms.
Schwarzkopf: 178 cms.
SS Records: 180 cms.

Guenther and Barbara Wagner: Wagner had 1938 appendectomy.

I hope these details can be of assistance to you in
your subsequent inquiries.

Yours faithfully,
(signed)
Assistant Public Prosecutor.

From that little lot, thought Steiger, you could take
your choice. The suspect may have lost all his teeth by
now, but the appendix scar and the possible scars on
the heel, forehead and eyelid were interesting. Steiger
noted them down for his next message to Bentor in
Rome, and the part about his preferring boiled food.
Measuring his hat size and exact height were going to
be difficult at this stage short of thumping him with a
blackjack or chloroforming him, both of which just
might make him suspect he had been found out.

The next document in the Wagner file Steiger was thumbing through looked as if the American Central Intelligence Agency had balled things up only two years after the war, when they were taken to the grave with Wagner's headstone on it in Berlin. They had opened up the grave all right, but re-sealed it when they were satisfied there were human remains in there, without making an expert investigation.

Only when persistent reports started coming in that Wagner was still alive was the grave reopened in 1963 and a post-mortem ordered.

The Berlin Forensic Medicine Institute's report showed:

1) There was no single complete skeleton among the bones examined,
2) there were bones and other remains of at least three people in the grave, probably including parts of a woman,
3) the one skull in the grave could not have been Wagner's as it belonged to a man who, at death, was only twenty-seven—and Wagner was thirty-seven at war's end, and
4) the jawbone found in the grave did not belong to the skull.

If only the Americans had analyzed the remains in 1947, thought Steiger, there would have been a better chance of tracing him before the trail went cold.

From 1963, Steiger tried to estimate the more reliable of the hundreds of reports on Wagner that had been picked up. Apart from several reports that he had been seen in Austria, the most convincing version seemed to be that he had made contact with the Russians in the last days of the Third Reich after Hitler shot himself in his Berlin bunker (or did he?). Colonel Wagner, SS number 128,430, was said to have bought his life by handing over all the Gestapo files he could get his hands on to Comrade Lavrenti Beria, the Soviet Security Chief who rivalled Himmler for brutality and who knew useful material when he saw it. Beria used Wagner to recruit agents among the German prisoner-of-war camps in Russia for communist East Germany. One German P.O.W., Dieter Muellner, now living in Stuttgart, had made a sworn statement that he saw Wagner in his camp before he was released.

After Stalin died and Secret Police Chief Beria had been shot for being more of a swine than even the Russians could stand, Wagner had apparently found it prudent to get out of Russia. He was next reported in Hungary in 1955, where he was believed to be reorganizing the police force in Budapest. Fifteen months later he was said to have shown up in Albania. By this time he was speaking Russian, Hungarian, Serbo-Croat and the main Albanian dialect, as well as his native German.

The man seemed to be a talented linguist as well as an expert baby bayonetter, thought Steiger, so Italian and English would have been a snap after that lot.

In the Albanian capital of Tirana he was thought to have been sorting out the Sigurimi, the Albanian Secret Police, for the tiny Adriatic nation's pro-Chinese dictator Enver Hoxha. Some East German delegations reported seeing Wagner in the Donica restaurant of the official Dajti Hotel. There were still reports of Wagner being seen at the Albanian beach resort of Durres as late as 1963.

After that, the reports became vague. He may have left Albania in 1964, and made his way to Istanbul to join former SS chums. Then he was reported seen in Transvaal in South Africa and in the usual South

American countries.

As Steiger well knew, all these reports could have been absolute baloney spread by Nazi counterinformants to throw investigators off the scent after the 1963 post-mortem proved that Wagner's was not the body in the Berlin grave.

There was nothing in the files to prove conclusively that Wagner and balloon man Kent in Rome were not one and the same person. And Kent was a worried man carrying a loaded revolver who seemed to fear someone would catch up with him one day.

Maybe, Steiger thought grimly, that day was not far off.

He prepared a message to Yossi Bentor in Rome telling him to tighten the watch on Kent, gave him all the extra physical details contained in the German report and told him to try to get a line on the suspect's diet. He had another look at the pictures of Wagner and "Kent," but neither one seemed to show any scars on the forehead—if there had ever been any—and no photographs of either man showed him with his eyelids closed for the reported eyelid scar.

He buzzed the Chief and went up to report the latest information from Rome, especially the part about the suspect carrying artillery.

The Chief said, "Can we spare anyone in the field to detach to this?"

"I don't think so. They're all pretty busy with the Arabs. We're stretched with all the counter-terrorism, but Ran Shamir in Stockholm needs to move on to new pastures for a while."

The Chief grunted as he enveloped himself and Steiger in cigar smoke.

"In that case, bring him in and brief him for Rome."

They were going to need more help in Rome sooner than they thought.

Chapter Seven

Ran Shamir patted the bonnet of the gleaming new Volvo 164 affectionately after he had pulled it into the driveway of the South Yemen Embassy in Stockholm.

All that training, he thought to himself, and what do I finish up as—a car salesman, and a bad one at that. For Ran managed to sell his cars at such sensational discounts that his Arab customers couldn't bear to turn them down.

But then Ran was no ordinary car salesman, and the Volvo he was handing over today was no ordinary car.

In the garage that morning he had run over all the final details with the two "mechanics" from Tel Aviv. The sad-faced senior mechanic described all the "optional extras" he had fitted, extras that would have made the manufacturers spill their aquavits if they had known about them.

"O.K.," said the mechanic. "It's all set. When you start the car now you will activate the timing device, but the car will still be 'passive.' We have allowed for one hundred starts before it becomes 'active.' On the information you have given us, that should be more than enough to get it into the right position."

Even the mechanics did not know for whom the car was intended. Under the rigid compartmentalization of the Israeli Secret Service system, no one was told more than he had to know. The mechanics had merely come over to do a job for a man they had never seen before. By tonight they would be airborne on their way back to Tel Aviv.

And the job they had done was to turn the Volvo into a very special kind of time bomb—a time bomb that would kill one special person.

With the intricate micro-circuitry installed in the car, no one at all would be blown up for at least one hundred turns of the ignition key. This was to lull anyone testing the car, before the "target" sat in it, into a sense of false security. No searcher would find any explosives taped inside the body or the engine of the car, because what the "mechanics" had done was to substitute parts of the car with explosives. The steering wheel and part of the steering column were made of high grade chemical explosives thinly coated with bakelite and plastic. So was most of the dashboard. The inside of the bottom of the petrol tank was mined to detonate at the same time as the steering wheel and dashboard, ensuring that what was not destroyed by blast would be consumed by fire.

After one hundred starts, the most machiavellian part of the "extras" came into play. The mechanics had also fitted a voice-reader, a tiny detonator inside the steering column which could "read" the voice of the target. This meant that only if the target was sitting somewhere in the car and spoke would the whole thing explode. Voice-prints are as personal as fingerprints, and the target's voice had been recorded many times at press conferences in Beirut.

There was one slight disadvantage. Unless the target was some kind of nut who muttered to himself, the chances were that at least one other person, the target's listener, would get switched off, too, when the whole thing went up. The designers hoped most of the blast would remain inside the car and that no innocent bystanders would be hurt—with the emphasis on the word "hope."

The Volvo was, in fact, a very nasty car indeed.

And to get it to the door of the South Yemen Embassy was the high point of Ran's two years in Sweden.

The people in the Embassy thought his name was Said Salem, the son of Lebanese emigrants to Germany. But wiry ex-paratrooper Ran Shamir was a thirty-seven year old Israeli, born on a collective farm near Petah Tikva, one of Israel's earliest settlements. As he walked to the door of the Embassy he thought back over the events that had brought him to be one of the Institute's smartest agents in Europe. Although his parents were from Russia, Ran was dark, with black hair and brown eyes. As a child he had played with boys from the neighboring Bedouin tribe in the days of the British Mandate in Palestine—and his Arabic was fluent.

One day in Jerusalem, two and a half years ago, a paratrooper friend of Ran's asked him if he was interested in "seeing the world a bit on Government business." Ran, with visions of boarding a plane for New York the next day, jumped at the chance. But it didn't quite work out that way. There was a long series of interviews in various shabby offices in Jerusalem and Tel Aviv. Ran's only foreign languages were Arabic and a smattering of English. When he was signed on, he found it was only at the same pay scale as any civil servant working in the Post Office.

The Institute had decided long ago that anyone working for them was doing it out of patriotism and not for money.

The second shock was that Ran was sent back to school. For six months he lived and ate in a high-walled barracks-like building near the Zion Gate in Jerusalem. No one inside the building was allowed to speak anything but Arabic, and with the influx of Jews from all over North Africa and the Middle East, every kind of background and accent was taught. The "students" were being entirely reshaped into Arabs from Syria, Iraq, Egypt, Lebanon and even from the Syrian and Lebanese colonies of South America with their special idioms. One man in the next class was being trained as a financial adviser of apparently Iraqi origin to a Persian Gulf princeling. The princeling had not yet been told whom he was going to hire.

Others, like Ran, did not know where they would end up. They were just busy eight hours a day developing their cover identities. Ran knew he was to be a Lebanese working somewhere in Europe, a staunch devotee of the Palestinian cause. When he woke up one night muttering anti-Israeli propaganda, in Arabic, he seriously began wondering which side he was on.

His instructor, when he told him the training might be going just a bit too well, shrugged his shoulders and said, "When we can train a nice Jewish boy so well he becomes leader of the whole Palestine movement we'll be able to make a deal with the Arabs—unless he gets confused and forgets which side he's on. In that case we'll have to kill him. So don't forget you're on our side."

Towards the end of the course, Ran also got crash courses in English and French. He wound up speaking both with appalling accents—but they were Arab accents.

Then there were the advanced weapons and explosives courses, an extension of his paratrooper training which was a pushover, and training in photography.

And in karate.

Down in Tel Aviv, David Steiger had almost flat-

68

tened Ran as he clapped him on the back with a hand like a soup plate and boomed, "That's it, m'boy, you're going to be a car salesman in Stockholm flogging cars to diplomats. And to Arab diplomats you'll sell 'em at $1,000 less than the nearest competitor. They'll love you, maybe even invite you over for tea. And I hear the girls up there are just great."

Ran arrived in Stockholm with an introduction to a Swedish car dealer who thought Ran was Said Salem, a pushy Lebanese with good connections in the Arab diplomatic world. The Swede sent him to the Syrian Embassy, where he had been dickering with a First Secretary to buy a Saab. Ran stunned the Syrian by knocking $800 off the price the Swede had been quoting—in Arabic. He told the Syrian his cover background, about the family living in Germany, hoping to move back to Lebanon one day, and said he was making the big cut in price "so you can tell your friends."

The Syrian took the bait—and the car. Ran sold another car to the Syrian Embassy and told his Swedish partner he would sacrifice his commissions on the sales to get in well with the diplomats. The Swede thought he was crazy but happily pocketed both checks. Ran did all the things a bachelor newly arrived in Sweden should do. He already knew the Arab cafe hangouts where he could find his "countrymen" and their left-leaning Swedish girl friends. He eased his way in, striking up casual conversations here and there and offering his cars at rock-bottom prices.

He cultivated a First Secretary at the South Yemen Embassy by selling him one of his now-famous cheap cars. The Yemeni was the man responsible for passing on messages from Yasser Arafat's Palestine Liberation Organization to agents in Sweden and the rest of Scandinavia.

After the sale, the Yemeni asked him to lunch and

69

two other Yemeni diplomats came along.

Lunch over, Ran took all three for a ride in his demonstration Volvo and hinted heavily that he could make a very special price for the two friends. It gave him an excuse to ask all three out to lunch two weeks later, and he took to dropping by the Embassy for a chat every few days while the sales were in motion. Inevitably, the subject of Israel came up. Ran knew all the patter and rambled on about the injustices suffered by the Palestinians. The Yemenis sided with the Palestinians too, as any Arab who wants to stay alive does. After the first few meetings they admitted they were directly involved in coordinating terror groups in Europe, and over a period of months Ran became almost totally accepted by the Yemenis and their Palestinian contacts. The talk grew looser in his presence.

One name he kept hearing over and over again—Dr. Wasfi Aziz.

Aziz was a very big wheel in one of the terror groups based in Lebanon, the Democratic Liberation Front, mainly financed by Syria. He was the Operations Officer of the DLF, and by all accounts a very smart cookie. At least two Israeli agents, one in Madrid and one in Cyprus, had fallen to his men's guns. In several commando raids into Lebanon, regular Israeli Forces had tried to drop in on the Aziz group, but the birds had always flown when the paratroopers stormed in. There was a nasty suspicion the DLF was getting information direct from Israel about planned commando raids, and Aziz was one of the three men at the top of the Israeli list. The DLF were also suspected of planting a time bomb aboard a Swissair aircraft which blew up in mid-air, killing all forty-three aboard, many of them Jews.

The Institute was not interested in talking to Aziz—only in killing him. And they wanted so badly to kill him that Steiger told Ran to concentrate on pinpointing

Aziz's headquarters to the exclusion of all other work.

After weeks of getting nowhere on pinpointing Aziz from Stockholm, it was Ran who first had the idea that if the Institute could not find him, maybe one of Ran's cars could. He put the idea up to Steiger—and headquarters jumped at it.

It took several more weeks of smooth talking and lavish dining to get the idea across to the Yemenis. He, a poor, exiled Lebanese, could do so little to help the movement. He was not really wealthy, but he wanted to give whatever he could. He dealt in cars and he knew the fedayeen needed everything besides money—arms, dwellings and transport. Did the Yemenis think that if he offered a car to the great freedom fighter, Dr. Aziz, of whom he had heard them speak so highly, this would be acceptable? Mind you, he would expect no reward or advancement, just the feeling that he had been able to contribute something would be reward enough.

The Yemeni First Secretary's eyes went into soft focus. Ran could see he had played his hand right. The Yemeni was thinking, "Perhaps I could let Dr. Aziz think that the car had come from me."

Aloud, to Ran, he said, "My friend, your offer is most generous. But you must know that there would be no question of your delivering this gift to the Doctor himself. Even I do not know just where to find him— but I am going to Beirut next week and will make a few enquiries about the acceptability of what you suggest."

Ran said he understood the situation perfectly and just a note to acknowledge receipt from the DLF would be quite acceptable—this was thrown in to dampen any ideas the Yemeni might have had about passing the car on to a relative or girl friend. The Yemeni's eyes flickered acknowledgement of Ran's perfect understanding of his mind.

Two weeks later the Yemeni called Ran and suggested lunch. At the restaurant were the Yemeni and a

Palestinian Ran had met before and suspected of being in the DLF.

He was.

The Yemeni said he had canvassed the idea of presenting a car for Dr. Aziz' personal use and had been told that, while the good doctor did not wish to be shown favor over the other heroic fighters of his movement, transportation was something of a problem these days. He saw no objection to accepting such a presentation against a receipt, and Ran would be duly compensated when the movement won its cause and Palestine was once again free. The Yemeni's friend was authorized to give such a receipt.

That's it, thought Ran. A carve-up between the two of them in which they will share credit for the gift in exchange for a worthless piece of paper. Because, if ever the Arabs did win, Ran sure as hell would not be around to collect his money.

Ran reckoned that with any luck the Yemeni and the Palestinian themselves would give the car a going-over —and the search when it got to Beirut would not be so thorough either, especially after a few of Aziz' acolytes had been driving it around for a while to try it out.

Ran promised to get the car as soon as his order list permitted, and today was the delivery day.

He had done the best he could—there was still the chance that the Yemeni and the Palestinian would give the car to someone else, or just flog it—in which case other Israeli agents would have to get it back and disarm it.

Before Ran walked through the main door of the South Yemeni Embassy, he glanced casually around. Somewhere nearby were some other Israelis right now, keeping an eye on the bombed-up buggy. But he couldn't see them. The South Yemen embassy guard waved him upstairs casually. Ran was expected. He took the Yemeni First Secretary out into the drive and showed him the car, all fixed up with seat belts fore and aft, head rests, radio, automatic drive, the works.

The diplomatic plates were already attached as Ran took off the delivery plates. He took the Yemeni for a short drive in the car, ostensibly to show him all the gadgets, but in fact to instill confidence. He let the Yemeni drive the car back to the Embassy. He was an appalling driver and had two near-misses. Ran managed to keep a fixed smile on his face as he remembered he had not asked the "mechanics" what would happen if the vehicle got mixed up in a common smash-up.

Back in the First Secretary's office, he got the Yemeni to sign the formal papers for the car. There was no secretary around, no sign of the Palestinian DLF man he had met in the restaurant. If the Yemeni chose to double-cross him and keep the car now, there was nothing Ran could do about it. It was legally the Yemeni's property.

The Yemeni gave him a receipt in Arabic, purportedly from the DLF, for "a Swedish car," without even the make or model number included.

Ran went back home but made no attempt to get in touch with Tel Aviv to tell them he had delivered the Trojan Horse. The car would be watched by others from now on, and they would inform Steiger.

Ran's orders until further notice were to behave perfectly normally, to go about his car-selling business and to stay out of the way of his Arab friends for a few days in case they discovered the bomb device and tried to lure him into a death trap for revenge.

Two days later Steiger told him the Volvo had been shipped off to Beirut. He was to tell all his Arab friends he was going on a sales tour seeking new outlets among the Arab communities of South America for a couple of months, and to make his way back to Tel Aviv for the first time in two years.

Chapter Eight

Ran peered out of the window of the TWA jumbo lumbering into Ben Gurion Airport from Athens. The plane was too damned big, with too many people on board, he thought. It made a tempting target for terrorists who were prepared to lash out at anything nowadays, because they couldn't often get into Israel. And according to the thinking of some of the terrorist groups, American airliners were now legitimate targets. Ever since Israel's rent-a-car raid by crack Golani Brigade troops in April 1973, in which three Arab terrorist leaders in Beirut were shot dead, the Palestinian guerrillas had been claiming that the CIA had helped the Israelis with the attack. The Israeli raiders had come ashore in motorized rubber boats and found self-drive cars waiting for them on the shore. The cars had been rented by six men with French, British and other passports who had checked into Beirut's Babylon Hotel some days before. The raiders belted around town, blasted their victims, and left the cars back on shore as they paddled off into the night. The six men with the funny passports disappeared too, and the owners of the Babylon Hotel, who also owned the Ritz in East Jerusalem, even talked to a lawyer about sending the unpaid bills to the Israeli Foreign Office for collection. The stricken terrorists in unison claimed American collaboration with the Israeli intelligence operatives who prepared the raid.

I wonder if they're right, thought Ran. I wouldn't blame them if they gave us a hand after getting two of their diplomats shot dead by Black September men in the Saudi Embassy in Khartoum.

Suddenly he saw the coastline of Israel come into view on the left side of the huge aircraft. There was Tel Aviv, and coming up below them the old Arab city of Jaffa, blown to bits in the 1948 Independence punch-up and now mostly a tourist attraction. Ran shivered with pleasure at the first sight of his homeland in two years. Tel Aviv was a sprawling, ugly city even from the air, but it was home. Well, thought Ran, nobody hijacked us or blew us up on this trip. Normally the orders were to fly on El Al planes whenever possible on the incoming trips. It saved the Institute money and the El Al planes were considered safer. They had armored holds, a protective door between pilot and passengers that could resist a bazooka shell and a couple of very hard sky marshals riding shotgun with .22 revolvers and dum-dum bullets. The close range weapons were designed to kill a skyjacker instantly, and the dum-dums stopped inside the target, reducing the chances of hitting innocent passengers.

But Steiger had told Ran to get back as soon as possible—and all El Al flights were wait-listed at this time of year. As the jumbo crunched onto the runway and the massive reverse thrust of the four engines braked the plane, Ran wondered what all the hurry was about. He had reckoned he would have to make himself scarce after planting the booby-trapped car in Stockholm, and welcomed the idea of coming home, where he could speak Hebrew again and see his family. But he guessed from Steiger's message that another job was waiting.

As the aircraft docked, the passengers were told to

stay in their seats with their passports in their hands. The plainclothes security men wandered through the vast cabins checking passengers here and there. One of them looked at dark-featured Ran and checked his passport over. Even in Israel he had to tell a convincing cover story about where he had been for the last two years, finishing up with the most plausible explanation of all. "I should come back here any sooner than I have to, with the travel tax up where it is?"

Green-bereted Border Guards stood at the bottom of the gangway with Uzi burp guns. There were more guards standing near the baggage collection bays inside the airport building.

Nobody planned a repeat of the Japanese suicide squad attack at the airport in which the three killers calmly unpacked submachine guns and grenades from their baggage several years before and sprayed the Puerto Rican pilgrims who had arrived with them a few minutes earlier on an Air France flight.

From the airport he called an unlisted number he had been carrying around in his head for two years. "Welcome home," boomed Steiger. "Go back to the moshav and have a good time. Your parents have been told you're coming and they're waiting for you. Take it easy, relax, and be in the office by midday tomorrow. By the way, say shalom to your people when you leave. You won't be seeing them again for a while."

"Big deal," snapped Ran. "After two years, an eighteen-hour vacation."

"Never mind, dear boy," said Steiger. "You wanted to see the world, and by God I'm going to make sure you do."

He hung up in the middle of a stream of Ran's fluent Arabic references to his mother's probable profession.

The next day Ran walked past Dizengoff Circle in central Tel Aviv and down to an address on Pinsker, making sure no one was following him.

He knew nothing about the Headquarters office on Gordon Street. At his previous meeting with Steiger he had been taken to the house on Pinsker set up especially for meetings with agents. This one had "Atastar—Import-Export" written on the door.

Steiger's horrendous handclasp had become no less crippling with the passage of time. He came straight to the point.

"That's great work you've been doing in Stockholm, my lad. Now we have to keep our fingers crossed about your Volvo. In the meantime, I know it's been a bit cold up in Stockholm and," he leered, "I expect you're fed up with all those six-foot blondes. So we're sending you somewhere where the girls are shorter, darker and warmer—Rome."

"You mean to get on to some of those sons of bitches that keep going through Fiumicino airport with suitcases full of guns from Tripoli?"

"No," said Steiger, watching Ran's face carefully. "I want you to get onto a son of a bitch we believe is Heinz Wagner."

There was nothing to read in Ran's face but complete incomprehension.

"And who is Heinz Whatsit?"

Steiger sighed. He had expected something like this. After all, Ran had been trained as an Arab expert, and now it was suddenly Nazis. "I don't know what the younger generation's coming to. Here's the folder, but for God's sake haven't you ever heard of Bormann, Mengele, Mueller, Wagner and all that lot? We've only been searching high and low for them for about thirty years."

Ran looked down at the folder. "A Nazi war criminal? I never even heard of the guy."

"Well," snapped Steiger, "you have now—and if

you'll do me the courtesy of reading through that file, you'll know just where we think he is."

It was Ran's turn to get angry. "So what? I should worry about some old Nazi fart when there are Arabs running all over Europe trying to kill our people today? This is something in the past, something your generation remembers. Ask anyone my age if they ever heard of Wagner. Bormann, maybe. Eichmann, I only knew who he was after our people caught him and brought him back here. Go out in the goddamn street and ask the first ten people you see who Heinz Wagner is. I'm telling you they just don't know. And you want to steer me off the people who are trying to kill us today to look for some doddering old fool from thirty years ago?"

Steiger lumbered to his feet and wrenched the folder open. At the top was a pile of photographs. One showed Wagner grinning beside a line of Auschwitz prisoners hanging from their thumbs by piano wire. Steiger's massive forefinger struck the picture.

"There's your doddering old fool," he roared. "And there, and there," as he flung the whole pile of pictures into the air. There were pictures of Wagner inspecting new gas chambers, watching lines of men and women walking naked to the chambers, watching camp orderlies carefully sort out the victims' belongings into neat piles—clothing, watches, money, gold-filled teeth wrenched from the mouths of the dead.

"There's your old Nazi fart who isn't worth looking for after thirty years. And those," his finger jabbed at the pictures again, "are Jews—some of the six million those doddering old fools like Wagner, Mueller and Eichmann made sure you won't see around Israel today. Six million, for your information, is exactly twice the population of Israel today, and three hundred thousand people here are extermination camp survivors. Where is your family from—Russia? These people killed twenty million there, too. Maybe," he snarled sarcastically as he spread the pictures in front of Ran, "you can see your dear old great-uncle Joe here?"

Steiger had done his homework. He and Ran both knew his great-uncle Joe had died in Treblinka.

Ran stared sullenly back at Steiger and stuck to his guns. "O.K., so maybe these people should be taken care of eventually if they're not all dead by now. But every day you take me off looking for Arabs is another day in which one will perhaps get through somewhere— and we'll have another Munich Olympics massacre on our hands. I thought I was supposed to stop tomorrow's massacres. I can't do anything about yesterday's. And that, to me, has absolute priority. And anyway, I never knew great-uncle Joe. That was Europe. That was something else. You know as well as I do that those people allowed themselves to be led to the slaughter. They thought they could wheel and deal with the Germans, buy their way out. The only time they put up a good fight was in the Warsaw Ghetto, about four years too late. And you also know that nothing like that can ever happen to us here. If we have to go down, we're going to take an awful lot of the other bastards with us."

Steiger was beginning to sweat with rage. He took a monumental gulp at a rapidly warming soft drink bottle and tried the quiet approach, but it just came out with heavy sarcasm. "With your kind permission, dear boy, we at headquarters will decide what has absolute priority. No doubt we shall still manage to catch an Arab or two without your able assistance. As far as you're concerned, you were due to go under wraps anyway after the car job. It may also interest you to know that many people in this country consider the Nazis and the Black September birds of a feather. The Nazis were

80

more successful than the Black September mob have been so far. Every time we catch one of these big bastards it's going to be a lesson to anyone trying to destroy the Jews today. No matter how long it takes, no matter where they are, we'll get them in the end. You're going after Wagner now for the sake of your great-uncle Joe and all the other great-uncle Joes. There aren't many families here who haven't got one.

"Furthermore," concluded Steiger, "you're going after Wagner because it's an order. Go and get some lunch, read the file and get back here at four this afternoon."

Ran slammed the file shut and stormed out of the room without a word.

Steiger looked up at the ceiling and decided the conversation had not gone too badly. He and Shamir had not come to blows. The main thing in this game was to convince your men that what they were doing was important. He could hardly blame Shamir for going off his rocker. The Institute had done everything possible to train him to eat, think and sleep Arabs. They had even trained him to be one. Now, overnight, they were trying to turn him into a Nazi-nabber. Steiger thought back to his own days in the South African army fighting Rommel across the desert. At that time many people knew something pretty nasty was happening to the Jews in Germany and Eastern Europe, but it was not until the Allies crashed into Germany and opened up the concentration and extermination camps that the massive scale of the Nazi atrocities was revealed.

For Steiger the news of the death camps had been a turning point. He had never been much of a Zionist, and after the war could reasonably have expected to go back and live the luxurious life of a Johannesburg white. But he suddenly realized that what could happen to the Jews in Germany could happen to them anywhere else—maybe in South Africa too—unless they had somewhere to go. So Israel seemed like a good idea at the time, and he emigrated to Palestine, where the post-war troubles were beginning.

And if it hadn't been for people like Steiger and Bentor in Rome (he was a Buchenwald survivor) fighting off the Arabs in 1948, the argument he had just had with Shamir could not have taken place, because neither of them would have been here to have it.

Don't know what the country's coming to, thought Steiger. In my early days here, the Jews were the good guys and all the rest were the bad guys—millions of Indians with tomahawks circling the camp. Everybody knew just where they were then. If you lost, you got scalped. The Arabs made no secret of their plans to finish off the job the Nazis had started. If they won, there just wasn't going to be a Jewish problem in Palestine any more. In those days Jews from anywhere in the world were welcome, especially if they could carry a gun. In fact the new State of Israel said that any Jew had to be admitted to the State just because he was a Jew. Steiger remembered asking a Jewish Immigration Officer in those days, when the bullets were flying in all directions, how he checked that new arrivals really were Jews. "Well," said the officer, "we figure that anyone wanting to come here now must be a Jew or a nut. And if the nuts are prepared to fight for us, they're welcome too."

Nowadays Steiger just didn't know where he was any more. In America they were making films in which the Indians were the good guys. And in Israel a lot of people were beginning to think the Arabs were all right, too. Why, even Friedmann-Yellin, whose Stern Gang was the terror also of Arab villages in the early days, had gone all funny. Nowadays the man whose agents killed United Nations Mediator Count Folke Ber-

82

nadotte in 1948 because he wanted to give back too much land to the Arabs was wanting to give large lumps of land back, too. And then the Shin-Bet, Israel's internal Security Service, had been picking up native-born Israelis, some of whom had fought in the army's toughest units, for spying for the Syrians.

And crime—God, the crime rate. As ex-premier Golda Meir had once said, "I'll never forgive the Arabs for teaching our Jewish boys to be killers." Almost every day there were bank jobs and rapes. With that and the soaring road accident rate, Steiger had a secret theory that if the Arabs really left Israel alone for twenty years or so, the Jews would do a pretty good job of eliminating each other. Nowadays the Arabs were so rich they could afford to parachute thousands of Cadillacs into Israel and let the Israelis kill each other.

Steiger shambled out of the office for lunch and an exceptional quick double Scotch to brace himself for the second round with Shamir.

Ran Shamir was having some second thoughts too. He had sent out for a quick sandwich and was thumbing through the Wagner dossier in a room near Steiger's office.

Steiger was all right. A bit old-fashioned, but a top operator. Why shouldn't he and the Chief have this bug about the Nazis? Steiger had let him operate pretty much as he liked in Stockholm, with a minimum amount of supervision. He remembered one of his earliest coups in Stockholm, when he had heard a bunch of Palestinians planning to knock off Israel's late veteran premier David Ben Gurion on a tour of South America. The big "public execution" of the old man, who was then well over eighty, was to have taken place at a press conference in Buenos Aires, and the Arabs picked for the job were to fly there from Copenhagen posing as journalists.

Steiger had arranged for the two gunmen to be arrested by the Danes at Copenhagen airport. The rollers on their typewriters had pistol barrels concealed in them and the butts and magazines were found in false-bottomed suitcases. Steiger had fixed it so the Arabs thought they had just had bad luck during the routine search before boarding the plane, and Ran had been able to carry on unsuspected in Stockholm.

And it was true, thought Ran, that the Nazis were still helping the Arabs. In 1962 Nasser in Egypt had given a very nasty fright to the Israelis by launching four ground-to-ground rockets, one of them billed as having a range of nearly two hundred miles—just about what it took to reach Tel Aviv and Jerusalem in those days before the Israelis swiped a lot of desert in the Sinai. It turned out that there were a bunch of German scientists behind the Egyptian rocketry, and the Israelis had to send the Germans some very severe warnings—in explosive envelopes—before they got the message and went back to the Fatherland.

It was also true that, for the time being, Ran had to disappear from his usual theater of operations anyway. So why not take a little holiday in Rome chasing a balloon man around?

As he read through the dossier, his professionalism got the better of his emotions. The balloon man was carrying a gun. There was no proof that Wagner was dead and the suspect was the image of the wanted Nazi. Ran read the dossier through carefully twice and wondered what would happen if it really did turn out to be Wagner. Would he be one of the men who brought Wagner back to Israel for another Eichmann-style trial? Or would the Institute just be told to execute him and leave a calling card?

Back in Steiger's office the two men eyed each other carefully, then Ran laughed and said, "So what's the weather like in Rome this time of year?"

Steiger breathed a sigh of relief. "It's great. And maybe by the time you get back you'll have learned to eat spaghetti with just a fork."

"What are we going to do to this guy if it does turn out to be Wagner?" asked Ran.

"I don't know. That's a decision that gets taken way up to the top. But I can promise you it won't be good news for Wagner. The main thing is to try and go on this thing with an open mind. In a way, your views on this being a bit of a waste of time are a good thing. It should make you a good deal more objective. Between you and me, Bentor is one of our best men in the field, but as an old ex-concentration camp hand he may just be loading the dice against the suspect. There's nothing in his reports to indicate that, but obviously it would be a great feather in his cap if this did turn out to be Wagner. Your job is to be the devil's advocate. I want you to go in thinking of all the reasons why it should not be our man."

They went over the dossier again together point by point. Ran was going to have to memorize it, except for the details that were already available at the Israeli Embassy in Rome.

For this job, Ran was to travel to Rome on an Israeli diplomatic passport as an "attache"—a very useful and vague word—and get further briefing from Bentor on local contacts and progress so far. The diplomatic cover was to help him take in a few bits and pieces of equipment, like electronic bugging gear, a couple of long-barreled pistols and silencers. Once in Rome the idea was that Ran should make as little contact as possible with the Embassy after the initial briefing in case there was going to be any nasty business in which the Embassy could not be officially involved—such as thumping aging balloon sellers.

Three days later he arrived at Fiumicino airport on a morning El Al flight with his briefcase full of artillery in the middle of one of the airport's frequent strikes. The baggage crews were refusing to unload the planes, and cursing, sweating tourists were stumbling all over the airfield carrying their own suitcases and promising each other they would go to Spain next year.

Ran was travelling light, and walked briskly off the tarmac. No one seemed to care where the passengers went as long as they disappeared without making trouble. Officially arriving passengers were supposed to walk into the ground floor of the airport building and pass through Health, Immigration and Customs controls.

But Ran wandered through a small door on the ground floor, and after strolling around a maze of corridors filled with busy airline clerks and ground hostesses, he suddenly found himself out in the street on the other side of the building. That was when he realized that he, a man with two guns, had entered the state of Italy completely unrecorded. My God, he thought, how many Arab terrorists do the same thing when there's a strike around here?

He took a taxi into Rome straight over to the Israeli Embassy after phoning from the airport. An Embassy guard was waiting outside the gate to get him past the Italian police guards, but Ran was put through the search routine inside the gatehouse despite his official identity documents. The guard had been told Ran would be carrying a gun or two, but even as they walked over to the main building he told Ran, "I'll carry this for you," keeping a firm grip on the briefcase. Very good, thought Ran. You can't be too careful. There was a second identity check at the main door before Ran was finally shown in to see Bentor, with the guard still standing behind him.

"Well," said Bentor. "It's nice to see you. How's Deborah?"

"Her second baby's due in a month," said Ran.

Bentor waved to the guard after the coded exchange and said, "It's O.K."

The guard dumped the briefcase near Ran and walked out.

Bentor motioned to a chair and offered Ran a cigarette as he looked him over carefully.

"Any trouble at the airport?"

"Hell, I could have brought in a Sherman tank and no one would have noticed," said Ran, and told Bentor about the chaotic check system there.

Bentor smoothed back his gray hair. "Well, if the Italians don't know you're here, it might be a good thing in the end. I was going to put you in a hotel for a couple of days but you'd have to show your passport when you check in and all guest lists go to the police within twenty-four hours. We don't particularly want the Italian police taking an interest in you, so I think we will put you in one of our apartments."

He pushed a buzzer on his desk and Zipporah Harel walked in from the next room.

Ran practically fell out of his chair as she walked over, giving him her best front and profile. Steiger had told him about her—but he'd forgotten to mention she was a knockout.

Through the sound of blood pounding in his ears, Ran heard Bentor say, "This is Zipporah Harel, my secretary." There was something about the way he said "secretary," with a slight pause beforehand, that warned Ran not to make any flippant remarks.

"Ran here will need a flat tonight for an indefinite period. You'd better cancel the hotel reservation and put him over in the vicolo Savelli place. It's right near the Piazza Navona and should do very well."

He turned to Ran. "Only two rooms with a shower, I'm afraid, but there's no doorman and your flat has a front and back staircase."

Zipporah handed Bentor some news agency tape and said, "Wasfi Aziz has been killed in Beirut."

Ran sat stock-still as Bentor read through the wire dispatch.

The girl was looking at him, but he was sure that neither she nor Bentor knew what his last job had been or even where he had come from.

He puffed quietly at his cigarette while Bentor read, and then said casually, "Can I have a look?"

The wire story from Beirut said that Aziz had been killed that morning when he stepped into his Volvo car outside the Haddad apartment block building in the rue Kantari. A young girl with him, believed to be his niece, was also killed when the car exploded. A DFL communique said "imperialist Israeli agents" had planted a bomb in the car overnight. The news agency speculated that Aziz might in fact have been killed by a rival terrorist organization. There had already been some pro-Palestinian student demonstrations in town and a couple of windows had been broken at the American Embassy. The funeral was to be that evening, with more riots expected.

Ran handed the story back to Bentor. "It's a pity about the girl," he said.

"Yes," said Bentor. "But that bastard had it coming to him—whoever did it." In the silence that followed Bentor and Zipporah both stared at Ran.

Later in the evening they both drove with Ran over to his new flat in vicolo Savelli and arranged to meet him in the Piazza Navona at the Tre Scalini bar in one hour's time—to get his first look at the balloon man.

Chapter Nine

Peter Keane grabbed a table at the back of the terrace of the Tre Scalini and ordered his usual Campari and soda. He had been needing it badly all afternoon as the Rome temperature soared. As he pushed the ice down into the drink with his fingertip to stir the mixture and listen to the pleasant tinkling, he looked around. The usual parade was going on as Italians and tourists strolled among the sideshows of artists, junk-jewelry makers and the balloon man. At a table in front of him he again saw the man from the Israeli Embassy whom he knew as Yehuda Katz, sitting with his blonde bombshell. Keane craned his neck and was disappointed to see the girl had decided tonight to hide her sensational legs inside a pair of jeans. But as he let his eyes travel upwards he got his reward. To compensate for the slacks the girl was wearing a low-cut blouse so tight she must have been shoe-horned into it.

Keane's eyes bulged out almost as far as the girl's bosom over the top of what could laughingly be described as the neckline, located in the center about an inch above where her navel must be. Keane made a leering mental note that she must, as he had guessed earlier, be sunbathing naked somewhere. There was no white stripe in the brown skin anywhere down the plunging divide. Keane went on peering furtively, telling himself that, after all, he was on business and this girl and Katz had been the subject of a report by himself to his boss at the British Embassy, Joe Burke. After a second Campari, Keane had decided he would just have to go over and say hello to the couple to try to find out who the girl was—strictly in the line of business, of course. Why should that lucky bastard Katz keep her all to himself.

Several passing Italians were also clearly of the same opinion. All of them did a smart eyes-right or left as they passed the terrace and kept their eyes riveted on the girl. She ignored them completely and went on talking to Katz. Keane decided to attack and called the waiter over. He had just finished paying the bill when Katz suddenly stood up. Damn, thought Keane, I blew it again.

But Katz leaned over to the girl, muttered something to her and started walking towards the terrace corner where it turned into the narrow via Sant'Agnese in Agone, alone. At the same time the girl was turning her head and trying to signal to the waiter.

Why, that senile son-of-a-bitch, thought Keane. Not only has he got hold of the best-looking bird on the square, he's actually making her pay for the drinks. For a second he thought of transforming himself into a knight in shining armor and coming to the rescue with wads of money—until his training got the better of his lasciviousness.

But as Katz had disappeared up the street leading to Keane's home in the via di Parione he decided to follow him around and hoped to strike up a conversation with Katz until the gorgeous girl joined them. Keane loped off around the corner as the girl still signalled for the unattainable—a fast-moving Roman waiter. When he looked up the via Sant'Agnese in Agone he saw Katz staring in the window of an antique store on the corner of the intersecting via Santa Maria dell'Anima about a hundred yards away. Between them was the balloon man, who had just left the square, too, loaded down with his hydrogen cylinder, trestle table, bags of balloons and a leather pouch under his arm. The balloon man walked over the intersection and headed on up the street. Katz was still staring into the antique shop window. As Keane drew near, Katz turned away from the window and started walking slowly in the same direction as the balloon man—which was still on Keane's way home anyway. The three men walked in line ahead, each separated by about thirty yards, Keane slowly catching up to Katz.

Suddenly Keane realized that there was a fourth man in the narrow street, sliding past him in the darkening shadows on the left hand side and closing on Katz very fast. As Katz reached the other side of the intersection, the man in the shadows caught up with him and suddenly raised his right hand.

The first shot, echoing through the alleyway, knocked Katz flat on his face as it hit him right in the back. The gunman stepped up to the stricken man and fired four more shots down into him, the flashes lighting up the alley like small stabs of lightning and one bullet ricocheting with a hum like a bumblebee.

The killer looked both ways up the street fast. He saw the balloon man ahead, and knew Keane was behind him, but otherwise it was deserted as the sound of music came from a nearby open window and the hubbub of the Piazza Navona could be heard again as the echo of the shots died away. Keane had been stopped aghast in his tracks by the shooting. The gunman ran back to the intersection as a car drew forward. Subconsciously, Keane realized he had heard a car's engine idling as he walked up the street. The gunman dived into the back seat of the car as Keane suddenly started to run forward.

The car roared over the intersection, not even trying to avoid Keane as he ran up. In the back of the car he could see the gunman waving his pistol menacingly at him. There were two other men in the front seats. All three men were in too much shadow for Keane to be able to make out their features. Then a door handle on the accelerating car whipped his sleeve and spun him round like a top. Keane fell, but managed to get a look at the back of the car as the driver crashed through the gears to the next corner and disappeared. It was a Hertz rental car with a Naples number-plate.

Keane dusted himself off and found he was unhurt as shafts of light from opening doors and windows pierced the gloom of the narrow street. By the time he had gone over the intersection there were about ten Italian men and women from a trattoria shouting and bending over Katz. From what Keane had seen, there was no way Katz could still be alive.

Someone turned Katz over. His eyes were open wide, his chest was covered in blood where the bullets had gone straight through him, and there was a massive exit wound in his forehead. In the light of a doorway which opened further up the street Keane saw the balloon man looking back—and then suddenly noticed him turn sharply and start walking away from the scene of the killing fast. He was the only person in that street who was not running towards the dead man.

It flashed through Keane's mind that the only two people who had seen what happened were himself and the balloon man.

At that moment Katz's beautiful girl friend came running up the street. She thrust her way through the gathering crowd and looked down at the dead man. Keane heard her gasp and then break into terrible sobs as she collapsed to her knees beside him, cradling

Katz's shattered head in her lap. Over and over again she gasped the name, "Yossi, Yossi."

That was an odd thing to say, thought Keane, to a dead diplomat whose name was Yehuda. Briefly he wondered whether he should try and help the girl, but then he saw a policeman running up from the Piazza Navona. He decided not to get mixed up in a chaotic Italian scene, and he also did not want anyone to ask him if he had seen the killing until he had had a chance to talk to Burke at the Embassy. Keane stepped round the crowd and walked briskly over to his third-floor flat in the via di Parione. He called Burke and they agreed to meet at the Embassy in half an hour.

He poured himself a fast, monstrous Scotch and took great gulps at it as he sat down and scribbled everything he could remember about the shooting, including the number of the killers' Hertz car. Fifteen minutes later as he walked downstairs and out into the street in search of a taxi, he heard the wail of an ambulance siren round the corner.

If Katz hadn't been killed instantly, Keane thought bitterly, he would certainly have been dead by the time the ambulance got there.

It was only in the taxi on the way to the meeting with Burke at the Embassy that Keane wondered why Katz had been in such a hurry that he left his girl to pay the bill so that he could look in an antique store window—and get himself killed by the time the girl had collected the change.

Chapter Ten

It was not a very comfortable meeting over at the British Ambassador's Residence at Villa Wolkonsky, one of Rome's finest residential buildings near St. John Lateran with superb rambling English-style gardens all around it. On the terrace, which was a riot of pink geraniums, sat the Ambassador, the Minister, the Head of Chancery, Burke and Keane.

The Ambassador, Minister and Head of Chancery had wicker-work armchairs. Burke and Keane were sitting facing them on rather uncomfortable iron garden chairs. The conference, which was shaping up more like a trial, had been called in a hurry as His Excellency waited for luncheon guests.

The portly, gray-haired, immaculately tailored Ambassador leaned back in his chair and joined his pudgy fingertips together as he stared off across the garden.

"I'm afraid this is not a very happy situation," he said, his eyes swivelling back to Burke. "What you are telling me is that Keane here is a material witness to a murder and we have not given the Italian police information which may be vital in bringing about the arrest of the culprits. It is now—" glancing at his wristwatch —"some fifteen hours since that murder was committed. Perhaps, Mr. Burke, you would not mind running over again the reasons why you failed to inform the

95

Head of Chancery about all this until this morning."

Here we go again, thought Burke. Always trouble with these bloody diplomats—the eternal battle between the Foreign Office and his Department. The F.O. always worried about their image and what would happen if things went wrong and someone discovered Keane had been an eyewitness to the Katz killing. A nasty diplomatic incident that would be, and knowing the Italians, they'd probably wind up saying Keane did it himself. As for the Ambassador harping on about "failing to convey vital information to the police," that was all cod's wallop as Burke well knew. What the Ambassador was really panicky about was the possibility of being found out and getting a nasty clanger marked on his file.

Furthermore, His Excellency was trying to give the impression that Burke, Keane and the rest of his office had been goofing off all night, whereas in fact they had been working like navvies. All the information was already logged with his Department in London.

A heavy, graying man in a rather baggy suit, Burke looked back at the three impeccably dressed senior Embassy officials and realized they must be feeling uneasy, too. If it came to the crunch they were going to be the ones out in front taking the rap. In fact, they were all in it together.

He took a deep breath and launched into his defense of himself and Keane.

"The point is, Excellency, that in view of the murdered man being on the Diplomatic List and being of no little special interest to my department, Keane here took the view that he should report to me before talking to anyone else at all—the Italian police included. My information is that Katz is an Israeli agent in Rome coordinating all their counter-terrorist work here. I believe Keane's decision was quite correct. In

96

order to report to me before possibly talking to the Italian police—and I'm sure you will agree, sir, that that was the correct decision—he had to leave the scene of the crime. Had he offered himself as an eyewitness there and then, I don't suppose we should have managed to get him out of the clutches of the Italian police even by now, despite his diplomatic immunity. If he had approached the police *after* reporting to me, I think they would have taken an even more jaundiced view of the whole thing. And of course the Press would have become involved, because the Italian police are incapable of keeping their mouths shut."

A telling point, that. The three diplomats moved uneasily in their seats as they imagined the headline. "British diplomat sees Israeli spymaster gunned down —was his presence a coincidence?"

"As you see from my report," Burke continued, "Keane and a man selling balloons on the square seem to have been the only people in the street apart from Katz when the killer attacked. The balloon man was walking away and probably did not see the shooting itself. Keane remembers him walking off pretty quickly, as he probably did not want to get involved. That makes plenty of sense in this country. So he is unlikely to go to the police, and he certainly does not know who Keane is.

"As far as withholding information is concerned, we did, it is true, get the number of the getaway car. I have been working on this all night and I have discovered that the car seems to have been driven straight out to Fiumicino airport after the shooting. It was checked in there by three men with Libyan passports who took off on the night flight for Cairo with United Arab Airlines. I have their names and passport details here."

He handed a list to the Ambassador.

"I think we can assume all the names are false. I arranged for a er private inspection of the Hertz car, and it was empty. We have also dusted the car for our own set of prints.

"However, as soon as I was satisfied that the killing was an Israeli-Arab political affair, I assumed we would want to be involved as little as possible—not at all, if we could possibly help it. It is true that if Keane had given the car number to the police immediately they might have flashed an all-points warning to have it stopped. It is conceivable that—had they moved very fast indeed—they might even have caught the men before they boarded the plane.

"You will nevertheless recall that the Italians are not at all anxious to catch these men. They merely become a burden to the State and an embarrassment. If I may remind you, sir, the Italians have stretched their laws to the limit to avoid holding any Arab prisoners they do arrest or to avoid arresting them if they are tipped off by the Israelis or anyone else. You will remember that they released on bail the two men accused of giving two English girl tourists a time bomb to carry aboard an El Al plane at Fiumicino, and when they got a tipoff about two Jordanians driving through Italy to France with a carload of dynamite, they carefully let the car get into France first and then warned the French police. We know that the Arabs have been threatening trouble to Alitalia and Italian embassies if Arab prisoners are not released. They went slow on prosecuting the Arabs accused of trying to shoot down an El Al airliner with a Sam 7 missile at Fiumicino, released the accused on bail, and now they have all disappeared.

"So telling them where they can get their hands on three more Arabs would hardly have them falling over with gratitude. We could, I suppose, now tip the Italians off anonymously about who the killers are. But I think the only thing that would interest them in our report is that the men are now out of the country and the police can wash their hands of it.

"Incidentally, I suggest an anonymous tipoff if we do anything at all"—and here he gave a wintry smile— "because I am sure we would not like it to leak out to the Arabs that our diplomats are helping the Italians catch their gunmen. The last time our Embassy was blown up here, it was by Jews. I don't suppose we want the Arabs to have a go at the new place, or even your own residence, sir. And knowing their funny reasoning, it's the sort of thing they might have tried if Keane had gone straight to the police."

The Old Man took Burke's speech quite well. In fact, he even sent for some drinks, something he had pointedly failed to do at the beginning of the conference.

"Well, Mr. Burke," he said when the Italian valet had gone beyond earshot, "you may be right in supposing the Italians don't really want to know too much about these things as long as they are confined strictly to Arab-Israeli affairs. And I agree that one wants to keep the Embassy out of the press in these matters. The fact remains, however, that we are in a situation here in which Keane has broken Italian law by failing to give information which could have led to the arrest of some criminals, and we have to decide what to do about it. What do you think, Ted?"

The bespectacled, shock-haired Head of Chancery looked down at his shoes carefully and said, "We have had some reports in this morning from Beirut. The Democratic Liberation Front there have already publicly claimed responsibility for killing Katz—or whoever he really is. They say he was an Israeli agent and that the shooting was in reprisal for the killing of their leader Wasfi Aziz, who was blown up by his car in Beirut earlier in the day. In my opinion, the reprisal was a little too quick, and the DLF or some other group may have been waiting for some time to have a go at Katz here. But from Joe Burke's own information it does definitely seem to be confined to an affair between Arabs and Israelis. I really don't think we should get mixed up with it more than we can help. There is nothing in the Italian press this morning referring to Keane or any mysterious foreigner hanging about at the time of the killing, so I imagine everybody is prepared to accept the matter for what it is. The less said about it to the Italians the better, in my opinion. The only other point is whether we should tell the Israelis."

Burke winced. The one basic rule about his kind of work was never to give anything away for nothing. The killers had escaped for the time being anyway, and there was not too much the Israelis could do about it. And perhaps he was going to need a little help from the Israelis one day. The names of the killers of Katz could be a very useful bargaining card—but only when Burke was good and ready.

"I would advise against that, sir," he said quickly. "If we do not say anything to the Italians about this, I do not think the Israelis should be informed at this stage. Once the information leaves our hands, we don't know where it will end up. And we could still get our Embassy blown up."

The Minister joined in the conversation for the first time. Burke did not know him too well, as he had only recently arrived from Moscow. But he had heard he was the sort of man who liked to play his cards very close to the chest, and after three years as a Kremlinologist, concealing information from the local police had become second nature to him. The local police in Russia were not very nice people.

"Excellency, I think that everything points to Keane's involvement being completely unknown. Without going into the merits or demerits of whether he should have reported to the police immediately, the fact is that he didn't. We are now faced with that fact. And I believe it would be most unwise to involve ourselves openly or anonymously at this stage. It would raise more questions than it would answer in the minds of the Italian police and their Secret Service. As Mr. Burke says, the Italians probably don't want to bring any more trouble on their heads than they have already with the Arab-Israeli problem. Why don't we just let sleeping Carabinieri sleep?"

Burke looked at the Minister with interest. His contribution had been short and to the point. None of this crap about sticking to the letter—or even the spirit—of the law. A truly pragmatic man who seemed to grasp essentials quickly.

It seemed to do the trick with the Old Man. He looked at his watch again and said, "My guests are due in a few minutes. Well, I think that covers it, gentlemen. We shall do nothing as far as the Italians or the Israelis are concerned, and I shall recommend to London that the matter be shelved."

In the car driving back to town Burke said to Keane, "Don't worry about them trying to drop you in it. It's always their way and we've talked them out of doing anything even more stupid than usual. You were dead right to come to me before doing anything else, and that's the way my report will read to the Department, just to balance off any old claptrap they might get from the Foreign Office side."

Privately, Burke sometimes thought to himself that the idea of himself and his men having a diplomatic cover was more damned trouble than it was worth. Far better to set yourself up in a separate shop completely away from the Embassy, and not have to put up with their pontificating.

"Let's have a drink," he said, jamming his car, front

wheels first, into a minute space outside one of his favorite watering spots on the via Gregoriana, The Little Bar.

As he and Keane slumped on the velvet green couch below the bar and tackled large Scotches, Burke said, "Katz seems to have been a bit of a twit on this one. You saw him in the same bar with the same girl twice —and we all know Israeli diplomats aren't supposed to have a regular pattern just to avoid anyone getting locked onto them like the guys last night. I'd say the goon squad must have been watching him for a few days before they moved in. I wonder what he was in such a hurry about, leaving his girl friend to pay for the drinks so he could nip round the corner."

While Keane and Burke were mulling over the killing, a couple in London had been taking more than a passing interest in their morning newspapers. Miriam Goldhill almost dropped her coffee cup when she turned to page four—the Foreign Page—of the *Daily Express* as she sat on the balcony of their Hampstead flat while her husband Sam grunted over the stock prices in the *Financial Times*.

"What's the matter?" asked Goldhill as he heard Miriam gasp and saw her staring at the page.

"My God, it's him, Sam! That Israeli diplomat we heard on the news last night had been killed in Rome is the man we saw on our holiday. Look, the Express has got hold of a picture of him."

She thrust the paper under Goldhill's nose—and there, staring off the page, was the man who had introduced himself to them as Yehuda Katz when they went to report seeing Heinz Wagner. The report said Katz had been shot several times in a side street off the Piazza Navona, the square where the balloon man worked. The newspaper quoted the claim by the terrorists in Beirut that their men had shot Katz. There was no mention of the balloon man or of Heinz Wagner.

Goldhill swallowed hard and looked at the short piece about the murder on the front page of the *Financial Times*. It was more or less the same—no talk about Wagner.

He stared at his wife. "What a terrible thing—it's unbelievable. But that's the same man, all right. I didn't remember his name until I read it, but that's his picture for sure. What do you think we'd better do about it?"

After Miriam's eagerness to rush off to the Israeli Embassy in Rome, it was her turn to be reluctant. "I'm scared about this, Sam. I don't like being mixed up in it. Do you really think it was the Arabs that did it, or could it have been—?"

"The balloon man?" Goldhill finished the unspoken question for her. "I don't know. It's an incredible coincidence, especially as it happened just near the Piazza Navona. I wonder if we shouldn't see someone about it here."

Miriam bit her lower lip. "I'm really worried now, Sam. We don't really know what's going on. We gave our names to the Israeli Embassy. Perhaps the people who got Katz have our names, too." A look of fear spread over her face as she clutched Sam's wrist across the table.

Goldhill was scared stiff, too. In fact, at that particular moment, you could have stirred his knees with a spoon. I wish we hadn't got into this business in the first place, he thought. Then Miriam added the clincher.

"Sam, if anyone's got hold of our names, they might want to shut us up like they did Katz."

Goldhill tried to think logically. "Look, Katz is only

the man we saw. He must have made a full report, so nobody would want to get us, because too many Israelis probably already know about the balloon man being a suspect. I don't know why Katz got killed. Maybe what the papers say is true—it's a bunch of Arabs and the whole thing's a coincidence. Even so, it is odd that he should have been killed near the balloon man's pitch."

The Goldhills went on talking in hushed whispers as if they expected someone to jump out onto the terrace from the living room. Later that morning he went to see his lawyer and unloaded the whole yarn.

Between them they decided that some official in England should be told of the Rome conversation, as much for the Goldhills' protection as anything else.

By lunch time the lawyer had contacted the Special Branch through a friend, and a large man with a little bristly moustache came to see them. After hearing the story, he snapped his notebook closed and said cheerily, "I don't think you or your wife have much to worry about, Mr. Goldhill. I'll make a full report of this and we'll keep an eye on both of you for a few days. Let us know if you're going away or anything like that. And I wouldn't draw attention to yourself by talking to newspapers or anything like that."

"Good God, no," said Sam. The very thought made him shudder.

By early afternoon, the Special Branch report had gone to the Department, and a copy was waiting for Joe Burke after he got back from a leisurely Italian lunch to the Rome Embassy. Burke called Keane into his office and tossed the report over.

"Now we know what Katz was doing up that back alley, leaving Miss Beautyboobs to settle the bill," said Burke. "And there's something else for starters. This report stays right here in this office—and there's to be no chance of the Ambassador getting his greasy fingers

104

on it and maybe lousing things up."

Keane finished reading the report. "Well, I'll be damned. Do you really think old Katz got so wound up following the balloon man around he forgot to watch his back and let the Arabs get their chance?"

"Could be," said Burke. "They get very uptight about these old Nazi war criminals. Remember what a song and dance they made about Eichmann in Israel? Wagner would be a very big fish for them. I see from the evening papers the Israelis are releasing a bit of background on Katz. It seems he was a graduate of Buchenwald. Come to think of it, the Jews have every right to want to find those men. I saw some of those camps in Germany when I was in the army."

"I wonder if that balloon man is Wagner," said Keane. "He certainly was in no hurry to stand around after the shooting."

Burke thought for a moment.

"I don't know if the Department is too interested in the Israelis chasing round after potential war criminals. But there may be some loose ends to look into. I think we'll have a couple of the lads bird-dog that balloon man for a while.

"At the very least we should be able to get a lead on what some of the Israelis' men in town look like. They're bound to put someone else onto the job now that Katz has been switched off."

He eyed Keane and added, "I know this is going to ruin your day. But your job is to find out just who Miss Beautyboobs is. It's a pound to a pinch of shit she works at the Israeli Embassy—but we'd just better be sure."

Keane grinned. "Now, that is what I call a real intelligence assignment. How should I handle her if I get to meet her?"

"Don't ask filthy questions," snapped Burke.

Chapter Eleven

Ran Shamir carefully unpacked his guns and ammunition in the walkup flat in vicolo Savelli and popped them into the wall safe thoughtfully provided by the Israeli Embassy. He also put one million lire in 10,000-lire notes in with them and dropped the key into his pocket. Standing orders were never to carry heaters unless you reckoned you might have to use one.

He checked the locks on the front and back doors, examined the rear fire escape, and "swept" all the rooms with the electronic gear he had brought from Tel Aviv. There seemed to be no bugs, and no one had mined the telephone.

The rooms were small, but there was a drinks cabinet, a television set and a radio which could pick up the Voice of Israel. All I need, he thought, is a bird—and immediately his mind wandered to the one girl in Rome he knew—Zipporah Harel. She was really something, but she seemed to be Bentor's preserve, so he'd better lay off that one. A pity really, because as she was top-cleared it would have been a very convenient arrangement for his few days here. Ah, well, the Service couldn't provide everything.

He took a quick shower, pulled a summer shirt and light-weight trousers out of his suitcase and walked down to the narrow street below after carefully triple-locking his door, six turns on the bottom lock.

As he strolled the hundred yards toward the "blunt" end of the Piazza Navona which Bentor and the girl had showed him briefly on the way to the flat, he heard a siren echoing in the night. The noise grew louder and closer. As he walked into the square the white ambulance swung in the wrong way down a one way street, blue light flashing, followed by a black Carabinieri Alfa Romeo. They disappeared out of the square again and he heard them rocketing along the road parallel to the back of the square as he walked towards the Tre Scalini cafe. A bunch of people were gathered near the cafe tables staring down the narrow side street and he realized that the police car and ambulance had stopped some way down the side street as the sirens were still dying down to a low growl.

Ran looked over the terrace tables. No sign of Bentor or Zipporah. He sat at one of the tables and ordered an espresso as he looked over the square. There was no sign of any balloon man, either. Everyone seemed to be looking up the side street, including the artists and hawkers.

He heard the ambulance move off as his coffee arrived, and the terrace tables began filling up again as the rubberneckers drifted back from the side street.

Some poor bastard gets knocked down or has a heart attack in the street and it's the biggest sideshow in town, Ran thought.

At the table next to him a group of American tourists sat down. One of them was looking a bit shaken as he said to his companions, "Gee, I got a look over the top of that crowd. I tell you, that guy had been shot. He was looking like a sieve, there were so many holes in him."

"My God, who did it?" asked one American girl.

"I don't know. Maybe it was a shootout between

cops and robbers—there are plenty of cops up the street now. But the guy didn't look like a bandit, if you know what I mean. He was kind of an older guy with gray hair. There was a blonde down on the pavement beside him making one helluva noise."

Ran's English was pretty good by now, but he still had some trouble with the nasal twang of the American accent. Had he known it, many Americans would have had trouble sorting out the accents at the next table, for the group was from Brooklyn. And as every New Yorker knows, you practically need a passport to cross the Brooklyn Bridge—and an interpreter once you get there.

But he had heard the word "shot" and he got the reference to "an older guy" and "a blonde." Inside him a warning bell rang. He looked out over the square again. There was still no sign of the balloon man or Bentor and the girl. They should have been here twenty minutes ago.

He leaned over to the American table. "Excuse me, ladies and gentlemen, but did I overhear you say someone has been shot?"

"That's right, sir," said the first man, who was wearing a technicolor shirt and about twenty cameras. "If my flash had been working I'd have taken some pictures. That guy was dead as a dodo. They'll be delivering him straight to the morgue."

Ran tried not to look too interested. "Who was the man?"

"Dunno," said the technicolor shirt. "Everyone was screaming around and talking in Italian. But he's been shot, all right. I was in Vietnam. He died so fast he hardly bled. He'd stopped one right between the eyes. And his shirt was a real mess."

"Did you say his wife was with him?" asked Ran.

"Don't know if it was his wife, mister. She was

109

young enough to be his daughter—real pretty, too. But she was in one helluva state, trying to shake this guy back to life or something, getting blood all over herself. She wouldn't get in the police car and insisted on driving with him in the ambulance."

"Poor woman," said Ran, as he signalled for the waiter with an increasing sinking sensation in his stomach. Zipporah was a blonde, wearing slacks when he'd last seen her. And she was young enough to be the daughter of Bentor, a "kind of older guy with gray hair."

He followed the waiter back in to the cashier's desk. The waiter only spoke enough English to get orders and prices reasonably straight, but the girl cashier looked a little brighter.

"Who was shot outside?" asked Ran.

"I don't know, but some of the waiters, they say it was—*come si dice*—a Jewish man."

Ran belted out of the cafe and up the side street. There across the intersection fifty Italians were standing around talking at the tops of their voices, each giving his own special version of what happened. As no one had actually seen the shooting, that made fifty packs of lies.

On the cobbled paving stones there was a chalk outline of a man's body and two patches of blood. Two police cars were parked on the street, their uniformed drivers leaning against the radiator grilles. And plainclothes detectives were walking around with flashlights, presumably looking for bullets or cartridge cases. Two reporters from a Rome newspaper had already arrived and were talking to what looked like the detective in charge beside one of the cars. Ran sidled over and, although he could not understand the language, there was no mistaking the words the detective was dictating to the two reporters.

"*Si chiama Katz, Yehuda Katz*," the cop was saying, as the newspapermen scribbled. And there was no mistaking another word he heard—"*morto, e morto sul colpo.*"

Yossi Bentor was dead.

Ran pounded back to the Tre Scalini, grabbed a telephone token from the cashier and dialed a number. It seemed to ring forever before a voice said, "Bellini Travel Service, can I help you?" in English.

Ran said softly in Hebrew, "Your client has disappeared and I'm afraid your chief sales representative has been hurt."

There was a pause, then the voice said, "How badly is our representative hurt?"

"In the worst possible way," said Ran. "His assistant has gone to the hospital and should be in touch with you shortly. I need two replacements immediately—tell them to bring emergency equipment with them—and get the chief sales representative's assistant over to me as soon as possible, too."

"Right away," said the voice, and hung up.

Ran walked straight over to his apartment and had just downed a slug of soothing Scotch on the rocks when the doorbell rang. He unlocked the safe, hauled out one of the .38 revolvers, and slid silently over to the door. Through the spyhole he saw two men outside, one young and skinny, the other thick-set and about Ran's age, thirty-seven.

"Who is it?"

"We've come from Bellini's with the equipment," said the older one through the door.

Ran threw the door back fast and the two men found themselves staring down his revolver barrel. "O.K., up with the hands and come in."

The two men obediently put their hands on their heads as they walked through the door. When they were standing with their backs to him in the living room he eased the automatics each of them had in holsters under their left arms onto the table.

"When do the buses leave for Fiumicino?" asked Ran.

Without turning or lowering his hands the thick-set one said, "Every hour on the quarter-hour."

It was the right answer.

"All right. Turn round and pick up your guns and help yourselves to a drink. Sorry about the dramatics, but we've just had one man killed."

The three men solemnly shook hands. Thick-set's name was Eli, the skinny lad was Shlomo. They told him they had already done some surveillance on the balloon man and knew where he lived.

Ran briefed them on what he knew about Bentor's death, which wasn't much at that stage. "We've got to get locked onto Kent again as soon as possible. He wasn't in the square tonight and I don't know why not. But Bentor's been shot, and we know Kent carries a gun. And from now on we carry them too when we're anywhere near him. You two get round to his address right away and try to find out if he's home. If he's there, keep a watch on the house. I'll arrange for relief later tonight. If he moves at all, stick with him and call in as soon as you can."

Eli asked, "So what if he tries to leave the country?"

Ran thought for a moment, and said, "If he checks in for any flight to a non-Arab country, let him go—we can pick him up at the other end. If he tries to leave for an Arab country you'll have to grab him—alive."

He looked down at the long-barreled .38 he was still swinging absently in his hand and added, "I'll need something smaller than this for walking around with."

"We thought of that," said Eli. "They're sending over a .22 with Zipporah when they finally locate her.

You know, she's going to be very carved up about his. She and Yossi had been having a thing for about a year now. I even heard a whisper Yossi was planning to get a divorce and marry her. But maybe the plan was more in her mind than his. You know, Yossi and I worked together a lot. I can't understand how he walked into this one. It's just not like him."

"We'll figure that out later. You fellows had better get going, we've lost an hour on this already."

The two men clattered down the stairs.

Fifteen minutes later Ran's phone rang. It was Shlomo, the skinny one. "The light's on up in his place and we've seen someone moving around. It looks like he's home."

Ran breathed a sigh of relief as the doorbell rang again.

Outside were Zipporah and the Embassy guard he'd seen earlier in the day. Zipporah was red-eyed from weeping and there were mascara streaks down her cheeks. There were ugly brown stains on her jeans from cradling her dead lover's head.

The guard silently handed Ran the .22 and a box of cartridges. There was a silencer, too. Zipporah sat on the couch and stared straight ahead.

"I fetched her from the hospital when she called in," said the guard, obviously relieved at shedding his responsibility onto Ran's shoulders, "and brought her straight over here." He continued quietly, "The Ambassador and Bentor's wife have gone to the city morgue, so I thought it best not to stay. A short report's been sent to Tel Aviv already."

Ran poured the girl a stiff shot of brandy. He'd read somewhere that you were not supposed to give people alcohol after a shock, only tea or something like that. But what the hell, she looked as if she needed it. Zipporah wordlessly took the brandy and threw it down at a gulp, wincing at the same time as the fiery liquid burned its way down.

She needed it all right.

Ran filled her glass again and then turned to the guard. "Look, I think we might need some blotting paper after this alcohol, but I've no food in the house and I can't take her out looking like this. Can you get sandwiches or something at this hour?"

"That's O.K. I'll get some pizzas. I should be about ten minutes." With that the guard shot out of the highly emotional atmosphere of Ran's flat and off to the Campo De'Fiori where there was a late-night pizzeria.

At the risk of her becoming hysterical, Ran decided he had to debrief Zipporah as soon as possible. He tried the gentle approach. "Zipporah, I am very, very sorry to hear about Yossi. I know you and he were very friendly. And I know how upset you must be. But I want you to tell me exactly what happened out there. We have to move very fast now."

Zipporah was holding her glass in one hand, screwing a handkerchief into a tight ball in the other. She suddenly brought her face up and the coldness of her ice blue eyes shocked Ran.

She stared at him blankly, shuddered and then began in a flat voice, "We were sitting at the cafe waiting for you. The idea was for you to get a look at the balloon man and follow him back home so that you would get the layout. I don't know why, but he packed up half an hour earlier than usual, before Yossi's relief was due to show up. So we decided Yossi had better keep an eye on him until you and the relief man arrived. I would have gone with him too, only I stayed behind to pay for the drinks."

She suddenly realized what she was saying and took another quick slug of brandy. "My God, if I'd gone with him we would both have been killed."

The ice in her eyes melted as tears softened them. In spite of the awfulness of the situation, Ran found it nearly impossible to suppress his longing for her.

"Maybe it would have been better that way. I loved him very much, you know."

Ran limited himself to patting her hand. "Don't be silly, Zipporah. One of you dead is already too many. Two would only double the problem. Now please tell me what you saw."

After a short pause and a dab at her eyes, Zipporah went on. "I'd just got the change when I heard some shooting around the corner. It sounded like five or six shots. I ran up the street and a lot of people were out in the street already—and then I saw . . . I saw . . ." the tears welled again, but she took a deep breath. "I saw Yossi lying there. The wounds were terrible. He must have been killed instantly. He . . . he didn't say anything."

"Where was the balloon man? Did you see him?"

"I . . . I didn't see him. There were too many people . . . and I was only looking at Yossi."

"All right," said Ran. "But when Yossi followed the balloon man out of the square, he was still carrying that leather pouch he keeps the gun in?"

"Oh, yes. He never lets go of that. It must have been him, mustn't it? He must have noticed Yossi before, but we'd always been so careful."

Ran had his own ideas about that. Privately he was thinking that if Yossi had been taking his girl out on company time to watch the suspect, she was a great attention getter. Even now, her face a mess and her clothes covered in blood, she still looked splendid. Even a balloon man—or a Nazi war criminal on the run— would take time off to give his eyeballs a feast on her, and that's when he might have noticed Yossi too.

But he couldn't tell Zipporah that—nor Yossi, now.

115

"Whatever happened," said Ran, "we'll soon find out. There's just one more thing. What did you tell the police about all this?"

"Well, I had to tell them who we were—I mean from the Israeli Embassy. But I didn't say anything about the balloon man or what we were doing around there. I just said we were out for an evening drink, that I was catching Yossi up and hadn't seen how it happened or who did it. They seemed to accept that. After all, it's the truth. I didn't see what happened."

At least she hadn't broken down completely and blurted it all out, thought Ran. Come to think of it, she had top security clearance, so the Institute must have figured she knew how to keep her mouth shut.

That didn't help the uproar that Ran knew grimly must now be going on in Steiger's Tel Aviv office.

He heard footsteps coming back to the front door and grabbed for his gun again, waving Zipporah back into the bedroom.

It should have been the guard with the pizzas—and it was. But Ran still demanded the password and stuck the muzzle under his nostril as he came in with the hot food giving off the delicious aroma of marjoram, fresh basil and tomato sauce.

He told the guard to go home and get some sleep and tore hungrily into the pizza. He assumed Zipporah was in the bathroom straightening herself out after her tearful report.

But then he heard a soft movement in the bedroom.

She could be dog-tired or she could have cut her wrists, in the mood she was in, thought Ran, as he crept to the bedroom door. Either way, it was his bedroom for the time being, and he had a right to know what was going on in it.

The light from the bathroom fell across part of the room and he could see the bed-cover on the floor. A chair had Zipporah's clothes flung over it.

Suddenly the bedside light snapped on. She was staring straight at him, her cornflower eyes still dewy from the tears, with an expression he found hard to understand. He could see the nipples of her naked breasts and the rest of her body undulating under the yellow sheet.

In a flat but commanding voice she said simply, "I need you—now."

That makes two of us, thought Ran, as he ripped off his clothes and moved over to the bed. This was no time for Freudian rationalization about why a beautiful woman whose lover had been murdered only hours before wanted to make love with an almost total stranger.

But, normally an impetuous lover, Ran gently pulled back the sheet and decided to be slow and considerate in taking Zipporah. The sight of her incredible body changed all that—and he reached out for her hungrily.

To his amazement and delight she was instantly ready for his embrace, moaning with joy at his touch and ready for him with every movement. In the warm night their intertwined bodies became drenched with rivers of sweat as their lovemaking went on and on.

Finally, they both fell back exhausted.

Her head resting on his shoulder, they shared a cigarette.

And Ran spoke for the first time. "I don't suppose you want to tell me why."

Zipporah murmured, "Not particularly. Perhaps it's because I don't really know myself. Really, the only way I get emotional release is through sex. Or perhaps it was the brandy. Then again, it may be something subconscious in me telling me I'm not going to sit around grieving like a nun for the rest of my life. Yossi wasn't the first—and now he's not the last."

She laughed harshly and said, "There you are. Now I've given you four reasons."

It sounded too tough, and it was. Zipporah burst into

tears again and clung frantically to Ran, not sexually this time, but like a frightened child hanging onto her parent.

Ran stroked her back soothingly and she eventually sighed. "I'd like to stay with you tonight. I couldn't face being alone." She accepted another cigarette. "Look, I'm sorry to use you like this, and I'll be in charge of myself again by tomorrow. Then we can get the whole thing back onto a professional relationship."

It was Ran's private view that the lady could use him the way she just had any damn time she liked, but he had a feeling he had just been dismissed.

He eased himself out of the bed and said, "I can't use the phone here. I have to go over and file a report to Tel Aviv. You get some sleep and I'll be back as soon as I can."

He looked down. She was asleep already.

He headed across town to the Bellini Travel Service to make his own report to Steiger.

It was two o'clock in the morning by the time he got back to the narrow vicolo del Fico where balloon man Kent, or whoever he was, lived. Eli and Shlomo were sitting in a car nearby.

"Nothing's happened so far. There's only one exit—this one—and the light in his room went out at about half past midnight," said Eli.

"I'll be back at eight o'clock," said Ran, "and the reliefs should be along in an hour."

"Don't worry," said Eli. "If this bastard's the guy we think he is and if he knocked off Yossi, I'm taking a very personal interest in his future. My father was in Buchenwald with Yossi."

As Ran got back to the flat and quietly slipped back into bed beside the warm and still sleeping Zipporah he thought back on his argument with Steiger over whether old Nazis mattered any more.

It was beginning to look very much as if they did.

Chapter Twelve

The atmosphere in the Chief's office on Gordon Street was glacial compared with the steamy morning heat creeping through the rest of Tel Aviv.

The Chief was sucking heavily on his disgusting cigar and breaking air pollution records with every puff. In the room were the Heads of all the Sections, including Steiger—with red-rimmed eyes from a sleepless night of coded telex exchanges with Rome.

Getting a man killed was no way to get medals in the Institute.

The Israeli newspapers and radio were going berserk over the Bentor killing. The Foreign Ministry had just made a flat announcement that the Cultural Attache in Rome had been shot dead in "circumstances which still have to be clarified."

But the newspapers were instantly jumping to the conclusion that Bentor was another innocent victim of the Arab terrorist campaign. Editorials were pointing out that there were a thousand Israeli diplomats and their families spread around a hundred countries and that most of them were sitting-duck targets for Arab gunmen because "the Security Services are not doing enough to protect them." There were the usual cries for retaliatory raids against the bases from which the killers had set out on their murder mission.

And on the radio just before the conference began there was a report from Beirut quoting a spokesman for the Democratic Liberation Front as saying Bentor was an Israeli spy who had been executed by the DLF in retaliation for the murder of the movement's leader Wasfi Aziz yesterday morning.

"Well, gentlemen, it's not a very good morning, I'm afraid," said the Chief. "I think most of you knew Yossi and realize we have lost a very good man. The point now is to find out just how we lost him and what we are going to do about it."

He turned to the Head of the Arab section, a dark, bespectacled Yemeni Jew who looked more like an Arabian Gulf sheik than an Israeli intelligence man. "In the first place, what about this DLF claim from Beirut that they did it?"

The Section Head looked down at his notes. "We are getting nothing from Beirut to confirm the claim. The DLF are very shaken up at losing their top man. According to my information, despite their public claims that we did it, they are assuming a bomb was put in the car overnight. Aziz was a careful man and I understand he had a man sleeping in the car in the courtyard below his flat all night. So they can't figure out how the bomb got in there.

"It looks as if they suspect treachery from some other group like Black September and the DLF are now giving the man who slept in the car overnight a very bad time indeed, trying to find out if someone bribed him to let them fiddle with the car for a while.

"So they are so preoccupied with suspecting other groups, or even the Lebanese security people, that I believe their denunciation of Israel was a matter of form. And when they heard Yossi had been killed they saw a chance of bolstering their badly shaken morale and claimed the credit for that, too. I'm waiting for further reports to confirm this, but our people have to be very careful out of Beirut at the moment in all the uproar, and it may be a couple of days before we get the full answer. And don't forget these people are quick to claim victories where no victories have been won. You remember the time that trench wall caved in on Moshe Dayan when he was out digging for archeological pots. The Palestinians claimed they had pushed the trench in on him.

"Also, they never react this quickly as a rule. They just aren't well-organized enough to get one of our men in Rome within fifteen hours of us getting one of theirs in Beirut. If they'd really blasted poor old Yossi, they'd have been on the air claiming responsibility last night— not this morning."

It all seemed to make sense.

The Chief looked at Steiger and asked, "What's the position in Rome now?"

Steiger lit a cigarette and stretched his massive frame in his chair, which creaked ominously. "Circumstantially, all the answers I get keep coming up that it's the balloon man that did it."

He counted off the points on his banana-sized fingers. "In the first place we know he was carrying a gun, so he had the means to do it. In the second place, everything so far is pointing to him being Wagner, so he had the motive for getting rid of someone he thought was taking too close an interest in him. In the third place, we don't know of anyone else being in the street except Yossi and the balloon man. There are no eyewitnesses. So this guy had the means, the motive, and he was in the right place at the right time."

"So what evidence have you that he suspected Yossi was following him?" asked the Chief.

"Well, nothing concrete. But I do know Yossi had been taking more than a passing interest in this case, being an ex-Buchenwald man. And I do know he had been taking that girl Zipporah Harel, our cipher clerk, around with him more than he should. Yossi knows how to fade into the background—but I'm afraid Zipporah is rather—er—striking. Getting her to fade into any background would be like asking the sun to set at midday. She was with him last night.

"And Yossi had been taking too much interest in the small details of this thing, too. His reports show that he was doing a lot of work junior men could have handled, like checking the suspect's diet. Incidentally, one of Yossi's last reports says the suspect buys boiling beef and chickens at the stalls below his house. Our reports from Germany say Wagner had a stomach disorder and preferred boiled food. So Yossi may have been moving in too close."

"Why did he kill Yossi even if he did suspect he was following him?" asked the Arab Section Head. "Why didn't he just disappear?"

Steiger stubbed out his cigarette. "If this is the man we think he is, knocking off someone he suspected wouldn't mean a thing to him. He may have thought Yossi was a loner—somebody like the English couple who first spotted him, doing a little private detective work. Maybe he plans to get the girl later, or hoped she would be closer last night. As far as bugging out is concerned, he doesn't seem to have the money to be able to do that. Perhaps he's decided that if someone is closing in on him, he'll make a last stand, whoever it is. When he finds he's blasted an Israeli it may be very small satisfaction, but he'll be feeling very scared indeed.

"My latest report from Rome is that up to an hour ago was still holed up in his loft and hasn't come out today at all. But then he generally only works in the afternoons and evenings anyway. But if he doesn't go out, or does anything different today, that's the last nail in his coffin as far as I'm concerned. All we have to decide then is just what we're going to do with him."

"Hold on a minute, Dave," said the Chief. "I know you've lost a man—we all have—but we've got to try to sit back and take an objective look at all this. If, as you believe, this man is Wagner, the decision about what to do with him does not lie within these four walls. You all know that the Eichmann law—genocide against the Jewish people—is the only civil law which carries the death penalty in Israel. And that means the Prime Minister will have to be informed and asked for a decision. It may be decided this man has to be brought back here for trial, or we may be asked to 'apply Israeli law' outside the territory.

"The Prime Minister does not so far know we are following a man we suspect is Wagner. I have been waiting for your people to amass a cast iron dossier. I must say it seems pretty solid at the moment, and I shall take the opportunity this afternoon when Yossi's death is discussed at the restricted Cabinet meeting to present our case.

"But it is paramount that we close as many loopholes as we can about this man. We will now have to take more risks, as the suspect seems to be alerted anyway. I am ordering crash procedure for all sections concerned. That means we are going to have to look over his place in Rome, get someone to look over Wagner's 'widow's' house in Munich for any signs of contact from Rome, we must get a sample of this man's handwriting fast and—ideally—we should try to test-fire his gun to compare with Italian police tests of the bullets that killed Yossi."

"That's another important point," said Steiger. "The preliminary police report in Rome says Yossi was killed at close range with a .38. One of the bullets found in him is in very good shape and there are powder burns on the back of his shirt. It looks like the son of a bitch waited for him in a doorway and got him in the back as he walked by. How we are going to borrow his gun to test-fire it, I just don't know. He takes it everywhere with him."

"Well, see what you can think up," said the Chief. "By the way, how's your leg now?"

"Good enough," grunted Steiger.

"Well, then, I think you'd better prepare to fly to Rome yourself on this one and take any help you think you'll need. I'll let you know the score after the Cabinet briefing this afternoon."

To the Head of the German Section, the Chief said, "Have we got anyone in Munich right now?"

"Not in Munich—but Shraga and Gabi are in Stuttgart, and that's only a couple of hours away."

The thing about a small outfit like the Institute was that the Chief could get to know everyone's dossier personally. He frowned at the mention of the two men's names. Shraga was an old hand, had been in the business twenty years and was one of the team that kidnapped Eichmann. But there had been trouble later between Shraga and Uri Haran, one of the previous Institute chiefs. While Shraga was based in Amsterdam as the senior agent he'd done a little moonlighting on the side—like opening up a small bank in Luxemburg without mentioning it to Headquarters. Uri Haran had blown his stack when he found out about it, and Shraga had missed disciplinary action by a hair's-breadth. After that Shraga didn't get any of the top-line security jobs. Although he was nicknamed "the Banker" by his colleagues, the outfit was still wary of him.

Gabi was a young lad just out of the Institute's finishing school for locksmiths, housebreakers, document copiers and other necessary little talents for graduates.

It was the fact that Gabi was a housebreaker that

decided the Chief.

"It can't be helped, I suppose," he said to the Head of the German Section. "We've got to get into that widow's house tonight if possible, so brief them to go ahead."

The meeting broke up.

Steiger went back to his office to draft new orders to Ran's team in Rome.

Ran had already been at work. Over the picture roller came a photograph of the electricity contract for the balloon man's attic.

It wasn't much—but it was the best they had.

The signature at the bottom of the contract was signed, Alfred Herbert Kent.

Within the hour, the two top handwriting men the Institute knew about were in Steiger's office. Of all the documents sifted through by Nazi-hunting organizations in the post-war years, only one had turned up with any writing on it by Heinz Wagner. It was an internal SS administrative document and also bore just a signature.

He put the two experts in separate rooms, each with a copy of both signatures.

After a few minutes he walked in to see the first man. The expert held up the Wagner signature and said, "This is a real, natural signature. In the second signature there has been a deliberate attempt to change the original style."

"So are they by the same person?" asked Steiger.

"They certainly could be. There is nothing to prove conclusively that they aren't."

Steiger could not get him to go any further. He went in to see the second man.

"I think these signatures are very probably both by the same man," said the second expert. "There has been an attempt to change style in the Kent signature, but the characteristics are both identical."

This man was a bit more definite than the first—but Steiger couldn't drag more than the "very probably the same" opinion out of him.

Bloody experts, growled Steiger to himself as he stormed back to his office. Every bloody trial I ever heard of you get experts for both sides saying exactly the opposite. One day one of these buggers would con a jury into believing black was white. Where's the Perry Mason spirit nowadays? On the T.V. they'd have had ninety-nine guys confirming the signatures were by the same man for sure, and he'd have been sitting in the electric chair by now.

He sent a memo across to the Chief fast as just one more piece of evidence in the swelling Wagner file.

At least neither of the experts had been negative.

Chapter Thirteen

Italy, thought Ran, must have the lowest alarm clock sales rate in the world. After leaving Eli and Shlomo watching Kent through the night he had reckoned to get five and a half hours sleep in his flat nearby until he took over the watch at eight in the morning. He set his traveling clock for seven-thirty. He need not have bothered. At half past six a man in the street below began trying to start his motor scooter. He tried and tried, the engine caught several times and sputtered out. Finally, after ten minutes, he revved the engine for another two minutes and roared off around the corner. Ran groaned and tried to get back to sleep, but an early morning walker below began coughing and retching before the unmistakable sound of an enormous gobbet of phlegm echoed as it hit the pavement, a health and accident hazard to future passers-by.

Then came the church bells summoning the faithful to the first mass of the day. "What will they think of next?" thought Ran as the peals echoed round the inside of his skull like a bullet trapped in a tank turret. "They're worse than the goddam Moslems with the Call to Prayer."

The Italian ingenuity for making a bloody awful noise at all times as far from exhausted. After the bells stopped, the hardware-store merchant below opened up

127

his shutter with a sensational crash and began hammering a round biscuit tin for reasons only he could fathom. Then the electricity company started up fifty yards down the road with pneumatic drills.

A recent survey showed that one of the six main reasons given by tourists who had decided never to go to Italy on a vacation again was the dreadful continuous noise, to which Italians themselves are impervious. In fact, if the Italians don't hear a noise around them they get nervous or think they are going deaf. Volume knobs on radios are clearly there to be turned up to the full. Otherwise the user feels he is not getting his money's worth. If two Italian families arrive on a mile-long deserted stretch of beach they will plonk themselves down within fifty yards of each other and exchange meaningless pleasantries above the din of their transistor radios and their squalling uncontrollable brats.

Ran felt beside him for his sudden, strange and stupendous bedmate. But there was only a cold and crumpled sheet and a faint smell of perfume where Zipporah had been.

Semi-conscious, Ran dragged himself out of bed, showered, ran a razor around his chin and staggered downstairs to the nearest coffee bar. His first espresso got his eyes open, the second one had them vaguely focusing. He walked zombie-like through the narrow back streets of the waking city to take over the watch on Kent.

One thing was sure. With this kind of noise going on, there was no chance the night watch had goofed off and missed any movement from the house.

As it turned out there had been nothing to miss. Kent had not moved and his light had not gone on during the night. But the night men had an urgent message brought to them by hand after being relayed to the Embassy from Tel Aviv by Steiger during the night. The orders were to get into Kent's lodgings at the first available opportunity for a discreet look around and to test-fire a round from his revolver for comparison with Italian police tests on the bullets that killed Bentor.

And Kent wasn't to know about either move.

Eli and Shlomo, who had gone off at three in the morning, came back to help Ran, and he told them what they were supposed to do.

"O.K.," said Ran. "Getting into his place for a look around if he goes out shouldn't be too much of a problem. Now, have either of you two gentlemen any suggestions about how we can borrow his gun, which he keeps with him at all times, fire a couple of rounds through it and give it back to him without his knowing about it?"

Eli and Shlomo both just stared at Ran.

From the end of the narrow street leading into the market square, Peter Keane picked over a few oranges on a vegetable stall and turned to his companion.

"Looks like they plan a big day," he said. "They've had two shifts of two men on all night and they've got three on this morning. Better nip off and call Burke and ask him to send one more down in case we all have to split up."

The third British agent had just arrived when things began to happen. All six men watching Kent's house almost missed it. From the rickety doorway of his building a man in a pin-striped navy blue suit with wide lapels emerged, the brim of a black trilby pulled down at a jaunty angle over one eye. The suit was something out of the nineteen-forties, the kind of thing with such large pointed lapels that the wearer could commit suicide by falling forward on the points.

"Who's that?" asked Ran.

"Dunno," said Eli. "He doesn't look like any of the people we've seen coming and going since we've been watching the place."

The man glanced both ways up the street and set off briskly up to the market square. All three Israelis simultaneously saw the familiar foldover leather pouch as he turned sideways-on to them, and noticed the familiar walk.

"It's him," yelped Eli. "It looks like he's trying to make a break for it in disguise—and he's got his gun."

Ran jumped out of the parked car. "Get on the blower, Shlomo, and tell them what's happening. I'll follow him on foot. You'd better tell them to be ready for him making a break for it either by air or rail, so we'll have to watch Fiumicino and the train station. I'll check in to headquarters as soon as possible, and if he moves far enough away we can bust into his place."

Then Ran moved up the street fast after his disappearing target.

Keane and his men were slower to realize what was happening, as they had not been studying Kent so long and failed to recognize him. But they saw Ran following a man—and then the penny dropped.

Keane dropped in behind the two men in discreet Indian file, sending one of his men off to call Burke and the other to keep an eye on the remaining Israeli agent in the car outside Kent's place.

That left everyone well marked, thought Keane. Much more of this and we'd be able to get up an Anglo-Israeli Secret Service seven-a-side match—and maybe ask the balloon man to act as ref.

The balloon man himself seemed to be in no particular hurry. In that strange old-fashioned suit he clearly thought he was rather nattily dressed, Ran figured. It was certainly not his balloon-selling outfit— and he walked all the way around the streets on the perimeter of the Piazza Navona and then headed east across the historic center of the city, taking care to keep on the shady side of the street in his thick suit, clutching the pouch with the gun in it under his arm and occasionally stopping for a look around to see if he was being followed. Ran and Keane were experts and he noticed neither of them.

Keane was in fact concentrating on following Ran without being seen, and leaving Ran to bird-dog the man called Kent.

The strange trio walked through the Piazza Montecitorio, past the column of Marcus Aurelius in the Piazza Colonna, and turned right on the via del Corso, the dead-straight main street of Old Rome running from the Piazza del Popolo to the Victor Emmanuel Monument, an architectural atrocity commemorating the unity of Italy known contemptuously as the Wedding Cake.

Kent walked up the Corso halfway towards the Wedding Cake. Just when Ran had begun to figure the man did not seem to be heading for the rail or air terminal, Kent pushed open a door on the street and disappeared inside. Ran hurried up and saw he had gone into the Foreign and Overseas Department of the Banco della Mercede. At a few seconds' interval both Ran and Keane wandered into the bank.

Inside was the usual chaos of an Italian bank. It was quite incredible how much talking the bank clerks were doing, how much gesticulating was going on, how many counter-signatures were being obtained from deputy-assistant-under-bank-managers, and how few customers were actually completing their transactions.

Dozens of foreign tourists and Italians were jostling at the counter. There was no attempt at forming any sort of line and being dealt with in order of arrival. The girl with the most garish makeup got served first and after that it was anyone who could break into the ultra-low attention span of one of the clerks. As in all banks, ten clerks were talking to each other well back from the counter and only two were dealing directly with the customers. Each of the two was trying to complete about five transactions at the same time and being constantly interrupted by the people at the desks further back. Every customer trying to draw money from the bank was being treated with the utmost suspicion. The fact that current account holders were trying to get back some of the money they had paid in was being treated as a hostile gesture. Banks, as far as Italian bankers are concerned, are for hoisting in as much of everyone else's money as possible and not for dishing it out.

In this atmosphere of highly-charged mistrust it was fairly easy for Ran to jostle his way up behind Kent as he tried to get attention at the counter. There was no risk of a clerk asking Ran "Can I help you?" and of Ran's having to think of an excuse for being there.

Keane also joined the melee.

After half an hour Kent finally got to the front row of the scrum and thrust a dog-eared identity card into one clerk's hand, asking him a question Ran could not hear. The clerk disappeared for around five minutes, wandered back, serving a couple of favored customers on the way, and eventually told Kent, "Yes, it's arrived. How do you want it?"

"I'll take it all in lire," Ran heard Kent say.

The clerk scribbled away for a while on a green form with three sheets of carbon underneath it. When he had almost completed the form he stared at it for a moment, pulled the carbons out, tore up the green form and copies and pulled a pink pad towards him.

Customers waiting to be served groaned, the clerk shrugged his shoulders as if to indicate that the forms rather than himself were to blame and had no doubt changed color, chameleon-like, while he was filling them in.

Ran could not get close enough to see how much was being paid nor where it was coming from. At the end of the form-filling the bank clerk handed Kent a metal disk with a number on it and told him to go to the cashier's booth.

If there is one thing Italian banks mistrust more than their customers it is their own personnel. For this reason, no single clerk completes a whole transaction. One man does the paperwork, another countersigns it, and only one or possibly two cashiers are actually allowed to hand out money. This is not because the men selected as cashiers are considered particularly trustworthy. It is just that they put up a bond on which the bank has a lien if the cash does not balance at the end of the day.

But the fact that Kent had to go to another counter to collect his money gave Ran a second chance. After another half-hour's wait the cashier called out "Two hundred and thirty-four," and Kent shuffled forward with his disk.

Ran no longer had any chance of discovering the origin of the money, but he saw the amount as the cashier carefully counted it out.

Somehow Kent, the man who made a living out of selling balloons, had managed to get himself sent one hundred and twenty thousand lire from somewhere abroad. It wasn't a great deal—about eighty pounds sterling—but it was more than Kent got out of selling balloons for six or eight weeks during the summer.

Ran's eyes wandered around the bank—and then he saw the calendar.

It was the first of September.

Kent folded the money carefully and stuffed it into a rear hip pocket with a button on it. Then he walked back out onto the Corso to the nearby bus stop. He boarded a number 56 with Ran and Keane close behind and rode the bus, after slipping his fifty-lire coin into the automatic ticket distributor, up the via Tritone, round the Piazza Barberini and up the via Veneto until the bus turned off at via Boncompagni.

Kent and his two shadows got off, and all three walked up the tourist-haunted avenue past the Excelsior Hotel, Doney's Cafe and Bricktop's. Hundreds of tourists packed the pavement tables looking around anxiously for the *Dolce Vita* celebrities the guidebooks said they would bump into on this garish clip-joint-lined strip of insincerity. No one seemed to have told them that the celebrities had left the street ten years before, chased away by photographers and rubber-necking tourists.

At the top of the street Kent bought a morning newspaper, crossed over and sat down on the terrace of Harry's Bar and loudly ordered a Pimm's No. 1. At Harry's prices that was about a day's earnings for Kent.

The balloon man stared intently at the front page newspaper story of the murder the night before of Yehuda Katz. "Now," thought Ran, "he knows just who he killed."

Kent sipped at the drink, which, to be honest, also included a pretty large fruit salad, and then walked into the bar and through to the telephone. He bought a telephone slug from the cloakroom girl and dialed a number straight away without looking it up in the directory or inside his gun-pouch.

He spoke on the phone for about five minutes and then went back to his terrace seat. He seemed in no hurry, sipped slowly away at his drink, read the newspaper again, and stared idly at passing strollers. Ran wondered who the only person Kent had telephoned in a month could be. His leather pouch lay on the seat beside him within instant reach, and Ran toyed with the idea of trying to slide the gun out and bring it back later. He had no idea how long Kent was going to sit there. He himself slipped into the cloakroom, called headquarters and asked for another man and a photographer with a long-range lens to be sent over right away. He also dictated a message to Steiger telling him about the mysterious one hundred and twenty thousand lire, Kent's odd change of appearance and the telephone call, and ventured the opinion that Kent was beginning to look like a man preparing to make a getaway.

He sent an order to Eli, still outside Kent's home, to break in undetected for a look around—and to be quick about it.

When Keane called Burke half an hour later from a cafe phone across the street and told him that Kent and Ran were still sitting nursing drinks, Burke said, "Another of their guys just popped upstairs to Kent's pad. He's still up there, the last I heard. Do you think he's putting a bomb under the bed?"

"I don't know," said Keane. "But perhaps we're getting rather near the time when someone ought to tell the Israelis Kent really didn't switch off their boy."

"Not a bit of it," giggled Burke sadistically. "Why should we stop the Israelis' fun, especially if this is Wagner? With any luck you'll have a ringside seat for the firework display."

Chapter Fourteen

While the man who called himself Kent sipped his appallingly expensive drink on the via Veneto, Eli was working his way through the man's attic and Shlomo kept watch outside. Although Eli was an expert, pawing through someone else's personal belongings still gave him an uneasy feeling. In this case, however, he felt no such qualms because of the enormity of the crimes the tenant was supposed to have committed, topped off with the near-certainty that he had slaughtered Eli's boss and friend Yehuda Katz. Eli reckoned that however careful people were, they invariably left things lying around in their own homes that showed a lot about their personality, if not their true identity.

Kent looked as if he might be a different kind of fish. In the first place, before Eli opened Kent's door with a bunch of skeleton keys, he looked around all the edges. He saw it at the top—an ordinary hair stuck between the door and the jamb with two tiny pieces of transparent sticky tape. It was just one more bit of evidence for the mounting dossier. Kent was a man who didn't like unexpected visitors and wanted to know if they'd been around while he was out. Ordinary citizens only fear burglars, thought Eli. And you don't need to lay little traps at the door to find out whether burglars have been in. They are very untidy people and they throw what they don't steal all over the place. Kent was worried that someone like Eli might take an interest in him.

Eli carefully stripped one piece of sticky tape away and left the hair hanging from the door jamb as he opened the door to Kent's attic. It was just one big room with peeling wallpaper and a window that had last been cleaned during the French Revolution. There was a grime-covered basin with one cold tap in one corner and a lavatory bowl curtained off with a gray blanket. There was an iron bedstead, the bed unmade, with sheets that had once been white but now matched the gray blanket. Hammered into the wall were a couple of wooden shelves with some pots over an old gas stove. There was a wooden table, two kitchen chairs, a wardrobe and a desk. The whole place was so filthy Eli was glad he was wearing gloves for the job. If this was the home of once-dapper SS Colonel Wagner, he'd certainly forgotten a lot of his Prussian discipline, like folding and washing things. Probably couldn't manage nowadays without his servants, sneered Eli to himself as he started working the room over. It didn't take long. There wasn't much to look at or many places to hide anything. It was what *wasn't* in the place that surprised Eli.

There were no letters, no books, not even a newspaper. The room was completely bereft of anything in writing. It would be impossible to tell whether the inhabitant of that seedy garret was English, Italian, German or even Chinese. Kent might be sloppy in his personal habits, but he was meticulous about keeping his background a mystery. Eli realized how lucky Ran had been to get a copy of Kent's electricity contract with its signature from a contact at the Electricity Company's office. Kent didn't write or sign any more than he absolutely had to.

There were not even any documents from the bank

he had just visited to collect his mysterious one hundred and twenty thousand lire. If Kent carried anything at all in writing it all went around with him in that pouch, along with his gun.

But there were three cigarette butts in the one ashtray. Although no one had ever seen Kent smoking out in the street, he clearly smoked at home.

Kent was a smoker—Wagner was a smoker. Wagner had been a heavy smoker. Three cigarettes overnight wasn't much, but people have been known to cut down on their smoking, especially with the cancer scare and —in Kent's case—the price of tobacco, Eli thought.

There was an old transistor radio on the table. Eli switched it on without moving the dial. It was set on an Italian music channel. Too much to hope it would have been tuned to Radio Munich.

There was nothing hidden among the man's few ragged clothes in the wardrobe, nothing under the mattress, nothing behind the gas stove or stuck under the basin or toilet bowl. The floor was tiled, and there were no loose or freshly-cemented tiles.

But there was another hair stuck to the window which overlooked a short, sloping Roman roof.

As there was nothing in the room anyone could conceivably want to steal, Kent was the sort of man who clearly wanted to know if there were unexpected visitors waiting for him behind his door at nights.

Eli closed the door as he left and carefully replaced the hair.

Then he went downstairs and told Shlomo to keep watching while he went to a cafe phone to call the Bellini Travel Service. They took his report and told him to join Ran on the via Veneto immediately.

Within an hour the facts that Kent booby-trapped his own door and window, smoked, and kept no documents or photographs in his room were on Steiger's desk in

Tel Aviv, together with Ran Shamir's report from the via Veneto.

Steiger managed to catch the Chief to add the information to the report he was about to make to the Israeli Prime Minister. Steiger drove out with the Chief to Sde Dov airport north of Tel Aviv from whence he was to be whipped by helicopter up to the Jerusalem Cabinet Meeting.

"I'm worried about his strange behavior today, especially after Yossi being killed," said Steiger. "What we got in his room isn't conclusive but it certainly doesn't disprove this man is Wagner. The fact that there are no papers at all indicates he is a 'read and destroy' type— the sort of man who gets letters from his 'widow' in Munich, maybe?"

The Chief grunted. "Let's hope she is a bit more careless about her letters and leaves something lying around for our lads when they call on her, like a letter from her old man or some evidence that she sent off one hundred and twenty thousand lire in the past few days."

"Come on. You know things are never that neat."

"Well," said the Chief as he walked over to the helicopter, "the Prime Minister likes things neat, especially when he's going to be asked for a decision on what to do about our man."

One hour later in the Cabinet room in Jerusalem the Prime Minister dismissed everyone except the Defense and Police Ministers and summoned the Chief of the Institute, the Chief of Staff and the Chief of Military Intelligence into the restricted session.

The last item on the agenda that day—but not the least—was the murder of Yossi Bentor.

The security reports were pretty gloomy that week. The Chief of Staff said that both the Egyptian and Syrian armies were now better equipped than ever before and that the Syrians in particular had new Soviet ground-to-ground missiles that could hit Tel Aviv. They also had a squadron of MiG 23 Foxbats that could fly faster and higher than Israel's Phantoms. At the moment the Foxbats were being flown only by Russian pilots, but Syrians were undergoing conversion courses in the Soviet Union. The Americans were dragging their feet on supplying the weapons the Israelis needed to counter-balance the new Arab supplies. After the disastrous Yom Kippur war, Israel's confidence in her invincibility had been badly shaken, and no one in the Cabinet room doubted for a moment that if the Arabs ever got a real edge in weapons systems they would launch another combined attack.

The Chief of the Institute went through his assessment of the battle against Arab terrorists in Europe and then lit another of his abominable cigars as he came to the Bentor killing and the Wagner file.

"Mr. Prime Minister—gentlemen—we have a considerable amount of evidence to show that Yossi Bentor may have been murdered by Colonel Heinz Wagner," he said simply.

The effect was electric. Even the Cabinet Secretary recording the minutes of the meeting, who had heard just about everyting in his time, froze over his pad and looked up.

There were no young Rans in the room who had to be told who Wagner was. Most of the men there had at one time served in one of Israel's security services and all were serving or ex-Army officers. Several had at one time or another been involved in the post-war hunt for Nazi war criminals. Every one of them would have considered it a privilege to be able to exterminate a man like Wagner personally.

The Prime Minister, a chain-smoker at the best of times, lit another cigarette while one was still burning in the ashtray beside him, brushed the iron-gray hair back across his head and told his Intelligence Chief, "I think we would all like to hear more about that."

The Chief went through the dossier completely—the Goldhills in London would have been stunned to know that their names were being read out in that room that day—and for once a roomful of Israelis remained totally silent.

As the Chief went through it all again it sounded pretty convincing. There was the striking physical similarity allowing for a more than thirty-year time span, the furtive behavior of the man, the fact that he went armed and seemed to be expecting an attack and—as the Israelis then saw it—the near certainty that he had shot one of their best men in Europe. After the Eichmann episode, the fact that the man was living near the poverty line was completely acceptable.

The Chief summed up. "So we are ninety-five percent sure this is our man. I am sending Steiger to Rome to check everything out again and we have the target under constant surveillance. We are going to look over his 'widow's' place in Munich—I hope tonight—and we are trying to get at his gun for a ballistics check. Quite apart from his being Wagner, I would have thought, Prime Minister, that the death of one of our best men would justify extreme action in this case."

The Prime Minister, a gaunt man with a slow, deliberate manner of speech, leaned forward and asked, "What do you mean by extreme action?"

The Chief looked around at the rest of the men at the Cabinet table and answered carefully. "As you know, in the normal course of events, someone who eliminated one of our agents would be taken care of without my bringing it up in this room. However, as the man in this particular case seems indictable under our Genocide Law, I assumed that you, Prime Minister, would wish

142

to make a personal decision about it. The problem is that a decision must be reached in a hurry because Wagner may be trying to escape. That would not be too much of a problem unless he tries to reach an Arab country like Libya where they would, no doubt, be delighted to protect him. He is already behaving uncharacteristically and has collected a small amount of money. He may have more money lying around and must already realize the importance of the man he killed. I was therefore hoping, Prime Minister, that we could get a decision before leaving the room this evening."

"If we wished to bring this man to Israel for trial could that be arranged?" the Prime Minister asked.

"Yes, but of course it would be much simpler to take care of things on the spot."

The Police Minister coughed and raised his glasses above his forehead. "An Eichmann-style trial here just now would present a tremendous security problem," he said. "Our people are pushed to the limit as it is, with having to guard the border settlements, and another trial like that would be the target of every Arab terrorist in the Middle East. Then there would be the fanatics among our own people who would want to lynch him and all sorts of other religious maniacs who would descend on the country like homing pigeons."

The other men in the room were also worried about the security problems of a show trial.

The Prime Minister listened to all his advisers and lit another cigarette. Then he said slowly, "Quite clearly, this abominable man has to be eliminated one way or another. On that we are all, I am sure, agreed. The advantage of a trial in Israel would be to bring home to the younger generation here once more what their fathers had to go through at the hands of the Nazis. It is more than a decade since the Eichmann trial and we have had two wars with the Arabs since then. People's memories are short, and they need to be reminded of these things. There are, however, some political considerations. To bring Wagner back here would cause us considerable problems with the Italians. To kidnap him on Italian soil would cause a major crisis, and Israel needs all the friends she can get these days. To ask the Italians to extradite him to Israel would be very risky—they might allow him to escape. We know their record for letting Arabs go, and there is a grave risk that during extradition proceedings Arab or Fascist pressure might be brought to bear on Rome."

He permitted himself a bleak smile and observed, "We know how responsive the Italians are to pressure. We would not want our man released on bail during the proceedings.

"I also take the point you have all made about the security problem involved in a trial here, and so I think that the advantages of a trial in Israel are outweighed by the disadvantages. This leaves us with the possibility of applying Israeli law outside Israel. We all know the penalty of conviction under our Genocide Law is death.

"In a sense, therefore, we in this room are now conducting the trial of this man and must act as judges, jurors and executioners. The Chief, it seems to me, has made out a very good circumstantial case against the suspect. I agree that it is ninety-five percent certain that he is in fact Heinz Wagner, and that is, in any court of law, beyond a reasonable doubt. In normal circumstances I would hesitate on the side of extreme caution and it would be far preferable if this man could be interrogated and a full written confession extracted.

"I do not wish to open old wounds, but there was that stupid mistake in Lillehammer when our people got the wrong man. That did our image no good at all."

The Chief winced at the reference to the Norwegian

episode, which had landed several of his people in jail.

"But as the Chief of the Institute points out, there is every likelihood that this man will try to escape, and he is already acting in an unusual way," the Prime Minister continued. "And so I am prepared to make a decision in principle. And that is that, if proven guilty, this man must be destroyed for his crimes against our people. But I make the one proviso that the Chief of the Institute must make a further maximum effort to establish this man's guilt one hundred per cent on either or both charges. Clearly a ballistics test on his gun would establish whether he has killed one of our men—regardless of whether or not he is Heinz Wagner—and that of itself would be sufficient justification for our action. But if he is Wagner, we will want the world to know he is dead. Naturally, the State of Israel must not be seen to be directly involved in the carrying-out of the sentence. I leave that to the Chief's ingenuity. But I must stress once more," tapping the Cabinet table, "there must be no kidnapping or execution of a man whose guilt is in the slightest doubt."

The Chief walked out of the meeting and over to his helicopter in a bad mood. The Prime Minister had rubbed the Lillehammer business in again, and the clever old bastard had protected himself very carefully if things went wrong in the Wagner affair. The permission "in principle" to execute Wagner was so hedged by the hundred-percent proof condition that a lot more risks would have to be taken. Kidnapping Kent to question him had also been ruled out.

Back in Tel Aviv he summoned Steiger to break the bad news.

"So that's it, I'm afraid," he concluded as Steiger looked off into a corner of the room, working out all his new problems. "The P.M. says we can eliminate this man when we have the other five percent proof.

145

The obvious way to get that proof would be to pick him up, interrogate him and test his gun.

"But the P.M. has ruled that out." Grudgingly the Chief admitted, "and anyway, that could all take several days and if, at the end of it all, we couldn't nail him, we would have to let him go, and he could have some very weird stories to tell. I'll want you in Rome as soon as possible—first thing in the morning—to take over the whole operation. Take anyone you need with you. There must be no mistakes."

Steiger decided he would take a marksman with him to cover any possible slip-ups—sniper's rifles were already available in Rome.

And that brought him to the last point.

Steiger looked straight in the Chief's face and said, "If it turns out to be him—how are we going to do it?"

The Chief and Steiger held a clinical conference on just how to put a mass killer to death. They agreed that a sentence of death by the State of Israel should be read to him. Hanging was used by Israel to carry out the only execution in the State's history—that of Adolf Eichmann. But neither Steiger nor any of his men was an expert at that kind of thing. Steiger coldly discussed the possibility of binding Kent and putting his head in a gas oven—an appropriate death for a gas expert. They thought of forcing him to take cyanide, so that he could die like Himmler and Goering. Then there was the gun or the knife.

Steiger suggested that Wagner's body, with his name pinned to it, should be sent in a crate to the West German Ministry of Justice with a note saying "From those who will never forget"—a bitter reminder that the Germans were refusing to extradite known war criminals for crimes in other countries and were trying to impose a statute of limitations on Nazi prosecutions.

It was the Chief who finally came up with the idea

146

that Wagner's labeled body should be dumped under the Arch of Titus in the Roman Forum. The message would not be lost on the world. The Arch commemorates Roman victories, including the destruction of the Second Jewish Temple in Jerusalem in A.D. 70. Only the Western, or Wailing Wall of Solomon's First Temple still stands today and is Judaism's most holy shrine.

The Arch of Titus bears carvings depicting the Jews being led from the Temple with ropes round their necks and Roman looters making off with the holy seven-candled Menorah.

To this day many deeply religious Jews refuse to pass under the Arch.

The Jews who were to kill Wagner would be making a special exception for a very special occasion.

Chapter Fifteen

Eli had just joined Ran at his table near Kent on Harry's terrace when the reason for the balloon man's telephone call became obvious. She got out of a cab and walked over to Kent's table. She was about five feet six inches tall, had long straight black hair, shiny black boots, a big bosom and bottom that shook as she walked, and a sharply attractive, heavily made-up face that looked about as soft as a bed of nails.

Kent gave his peculiar grimace that passed for a smile as she walked over and kissed her outstretched hand as she sank into the chair beside him and everything stopped shaking after a couple of seconds. Her low-cut blouse revealed a tanned and heaving bosom and her dark eyes flashed at all the tables nearby. She obviously liked, and got, the full attention of men in a very direct way. The waiter's eyes were glued to the neckline as Kent ordered another Pimm's No. 1 for himself and a Campari for the girl.

Kent started talking to her, leaning over and patting her on the knee, but the only part of the conversation—in Italian—Eli could catch was her greeting. "Well, where have you been all this time?"

At their nearby tables, the British and the two Israeli agents were wondering where this heaving mass of Italian flesh fitted into the picture.

Ran flashed through the Kent/Wagner dossier in his mind. The woman was not thirty—much too young to have any connection with the Nazi days. Apart from the fact that she was obviously Italian, the way Kent's hand lingered on her kneecap ruled out her being some kind of a relative. They had not see each other for some time. Certainly not during the four weeks Kent had been under close scrutiny by the Israelis.

The girl looked like a hooker, or at least a good-time girl. But she could also be a vital link in an escape chain Kent had had a couple of decades to work on.

While Ran tried to work it all out, Kent suddenly signaled the waiter for his bill, paid what must have been two days' earnings selling balloons and stood up with the girl. They made a strange pair as they walked off round the corner, a dozen pairs of passing eyes focusing on her shuddering anatomy while Kent in his old-fashioned suit grasped her by one arm, keeping his leahter pouch tucked firmly under his armpit. They left the via Veneto and walked down the via Porta Pinciana running just inside the ancient city walls until they reached the via Ludovisi three blocks away. They turned sharply left and walked straight into the front entrance of the Eden Hotel, a quietly expensive place with one of the best views of Rome from the Roof Bar and restaurant.

The balloon man and the girl, watched closely by the three men following them, walked past the reception desk, up a short flight of steps into the main lobby and over to an elevator. Eli, Ran and Keane, from different vantage points, saw the indicator stop at the top floor— the Roof Bar.

Keane let the two Israelis take the car up alone when it came down again, and put a quick call through to Burke from the lobby to tell him what was happening.

Burke said, "Keep after them—and if the balloon

man and his girl start getting crocked at the bar, don't join the fun. Our budget won't stand the pace."

"You're just lucky I haven't been given time yet to get after that blonde friend of the late Yehuda Katz," snapped Keane. "That could be an expense account you'll want to frame."

He cut in on Burke's rude rejoinder to ask him to send another man over to watch the hotel from downstairs, and took the lift up to the roof himself.

It was one-fifteen and diners were already sitting out on the flowered roof terrace with Rome spread out below them. Kent and his girl were sitting in an alcove at the bar end of the terrace and the two Israeli agents were in the next alcove. Keane sidled up to the bar and ordered himself a Scotch. Kent had called for the menu and was now giving orders to the maitre-d' as he sipped his third Pimm's of the morning and the girl tackled another Campari.

Keane heard the order. For Kent it was to be tonnarelli alla Charles, a kind of flat pasta with tomato sauce, ham, cheese and green peas. For the girl it was a special concoction of the house of rice, smoked salmon and vodka. Then they were to split a filet of beef with onions and wash it all down with a 1967 Barolo.

The way Keane saw it, Kent would not be expecting too much change from twenty pounds for his tete-a-tete snack.

But he certainly enjoyed it. As the aperitifs and wine took effect Kent's usually gray cheeks took on a pink flush and the girl began giggling loudly. After the beef there were wild strawberries, ice cream and a couple of brandies. At three o'clock the couple got uncertainly to their feet.

Keane had been right about the bill, but Kent paid without batting an eyelid.

During the meal one of the Israeli agents had also

left the roof garden to pick the couple up when they went down in the lift. At no time had they been able to get at Kent's leather pouch, which he had kept anchored between himself and the girl while they ate.

Back down in the street Kent turned to the girl and said, "So now, let's go," and they walked off down via Francesco Crispi for fifty yards. Suddenly they turned into an entranceway and disappeared. Keane and his assistant hung back in the street as the Israelis also hesitated uncertainly. The entranceway the couple had turned into was dark, but at the end of the hallway, a light was shining inside a porter's lodge. The porter, a florid man of about sixty, was reading a book of comic strips, his lips moving slowly as he read the balloons. He did not even look up when Kent and the girl passed him on the way to the lift.

Three hours later Kent came down in the lift again, this time alone. He still had the leather pouch, looked quickly both ways up the street, adjusted his hat and walked off toward the center of Rome. To all their utter surprises, the Israelis and the British saw him go back to his shabby attic and finally switch off the light at ten o'clock that night.

Ran decided to take a calculated risk. He had to know for sure what the girl was all about. She looked like a whore for sure—but what better cover for a hunted man to spend three hours alone with her working out the details of an escape. Ran was under orders not to grab Kent at this stage—but no one had said anything about not questioning anyone else.

At that moment the girl was at the top of the list—a list which, in fact, only had her name on it.

Rome has a funny way of shutting itself up at nights. In many old apartment buildings, the porter just came out and slammed the door at nine o'clock every night. Tenants had keys to the main door and to their own apartments. Sometimes there were not even any bell-pushes outside the main door, so visitors at night had to telephone people inside to come down and open the main door for them.

Other blocks had bell-pushes outside in the normal way and flat dwellers let their visitors in by a buzzer from their flat down to the main door.

Ran and Eli were out of luck. The main door to the building the girl had led Kent to was the first kind. No name-plates, no bell-pushes.

It took Eli about fifteen minutes to work over the Yale-type lock on the main door, and he was sweating slightly as the catch finally slipped. They peered inside down the darkened hallway. The porter had slammed his front office shut for the day, and they could hear a television set blaring away inside. Ran and Eli crept along the dingy hallway which might have been swept during Emperor Hadrian's reign, and slid into the creaky glass and wooden lift to the left of the porter's room. There were five floors.

The two men rode up to the top floor and got out into a darkened landing. There were the doors to three flats on the landing—and if the rest of the floors were the same, that meant Kent's girl friend could be in any one of fifteen apartments. Using a key ring flashlight, Eli and Ran worked their way slowly down the stair-case examining all the doors. Some of the bells had name-plates, but two had nothing. Ran ruled out the first two floors, as their name-plates showed they were small offices. He ruled out all the others that listed men's names or Mr. & Mrs.

There were no helpful name-plates like "Helga, Nazi Agent" or "Fifi, Swedish Masseuse."

That left the two doors without any name-plates and two other doors that just had Italian surnames on them —"Aureli" and "Di Giovanni" on the third and fifth

153

floors. Ran and Eli were standing near the elevator shaft on he ground floor, working out which door to try first, when a door opened on the third floor and all the hall lights went on. Ran bounded over and summoned the lift which they had left on the fifth floor. As the cage came down they looked around casually as the person who had left the third floor flat walked down the stairs.

It was Kent's girl friend.

Eli nodded politely and said, *"Buona sera."* The girl ignored them and flounced on down the hallway to the main door. By this time, the elevator had arrived and Eli and Ran did a polite Gaston-and-Alphonse act ushering each other into it to waste as much time as possible.

The girl was not going out. The agent outside would have picked her up if she had.

She opened the main door and the men could hear her greeting a man in Italian. As the door slammed and the couple headed back down the scruffy hallway, Ran pushed the button for the fifth floor. As they rode past the third floor they saw the door of the flat labelled "Aureli" was ajar.

The lift went back down again after Eli and Ran got out and rose again to the third floor as they peered over the banisters. The girl got out with a chubby white-haired Italian of about fifty-five, neatly dressed in a businessman's dark suit and carrying a briefcase, ushered him into her apartment and slammed the door.

It was ten-thirty.

It took about an hour. At eleven-thirty the door opened again as the two Israelis watched from above, the Italian pecked the girl's cheek and said, *"Ciao, carina,* I'll call you next week." When the girl's visitor, an eminent lawyer and nobleman whose family had given Italy two Popes in the past, got home to his wife and family in a seventeenth-century central Rome Palazzo he would have been staggered to learn that an Israeli secret service agent had followed him there and rushed his name back to Eli and Ran. Count Peroli was sure no one knew about his weekly assignations.

At one o'clock in the morning, Eli eased the door of the girl's flat open—his third bit of illegal entry in the past twenty-four hours. The two Israelis pulled stocking masks over their heads and stood inside quietly after closing the door. Ran's flashlight flickered over the small living room. On the right was an open door leading to a kitchen. Straight ahead was a closed door which they opened stealthily. The bedroom light was on, and the round bed covered in pink sheets was in total chaos. Lying at the foot of the bed were the girl's shiny black boots, some rope and a bamboo cane. Through the doorway to the bathroom the men could hear a shower running and the girl humming to herself.

Eli and Ran did not want any screaming in the dead of night. They waited on each side of the bathroom door as the girl finished her toilet and brushed her teeth. Then she walked back into the bedroom stark naked.

Eli's hand shot over her mouth as he moved in quickly behind her, yanking one wrist up behind her back. Ran pushed his pistol with the bulbous silencer on it straight at her left eye, leaving a couple of inches space so she could focus on exactly what it was.

She'd taken off the garish makeup and her face was covered with night cream. Maybe she was more than thirty at that, thought Ran. Her eyes bulged with horror and he could hear a muffled whimpering noise as she tried to scream through Eli's massive gloved paw. Eli hissed in her ear. "If you play your cards right, darling, you may live. The right way to play cards just now is not to scream when I let go. Because if you do, that thing my friend is pointing at your eye is going to go off with a sickening plop. It's got a silencer on it so no one will hear. And your brains will be strawberry jam all over the ceiling. Got it? Nod if you understand."

The girl stopped trying to scream, but she was clearly still terrified as her bosom heaved. The bosom and everything else fulfilled the promise it had shown on the via Veneto.

Then she nodded. As Eli slowly released his hand from her mouth she tried to cover her nakedness with her one free hand. Her kind of nakedness would have needed several big hands, and she made a very poor job of it.

Regretfully Ran reached for a dressing gown lying on the bed and threw it over to her. As Eli let go her other hand, she was so busy wrenching the robe around her body that she even forgot to attempt to scream. Then she suddenly started sobbing and collapsed onto the bed.

"Please, please don't kill me," she begged. "I've got some money over there in my bag. You can have it all. I'll get you more. But please don't hurt me."

Ran got the message, but his Italian was still spotty. He decided to let Eli do the talking while he played the sinister silent part. Without a word he grabbed the bag and turned it out on the bed. There was one hundred thousand lire and some small change, the usual cosmetic stuff, a bunch of keys, a small black notebook and an Italian identity card.

The card said the girl's name was Angela Di Pozzo, that she was born at Salerno thirty-two years ago and that she lived at an address in Parioli. So this flat was her place of business.

Eli looked down at the black boots, the cane and the rope.

"A guy could have a really nice time up here with

you," he leered. "Especially if he was the type that likes kinky boots and a spot of flagellation, eh?"

The girl stopped sobbing suddenly and looked sharply at Eli. "Who the hell are you anyway?" she snapped. "If you're cops, don't think this sort of thing will get you anywhere. I've got some very good friends."

Eli leaned over and slapped the girl hard across the face. "Belt up. When it's your turn to ask questions, we'll let you know."

The fear came back into the girl's eyes as she nursed her cheek. Eli flipped through the address book. There were a lot of names, all men. None of them was Kent or Wagner, but one was Count Giovanni Peroli.

"Who's the guy who left here at eleven-thirty?" demanded Eli.

The girl started whining again. "Look, fellows, I make a living, and I don't cause any trouble. If you want some fun we can all have a bit of a giggle here right now." She looked up at both men and wiggled her hips invitingly.

The two Israelis stood there silently, staring back at her.

The girl licked her lips nervously. She was beginning to be afraid that her masked visitors weren't interested in sex or money.

Eli said again, slowly, "You didn't answer my question."

"Look," said the girl. "You know how it is. Guys pass my name on to their friends and they just call me up. They all give phony names anyway. How the hell do I know who they are? Their money's all right, and I don't take checks."

"What name does that man who just left give you when he comes round for a whipping session?" said Eli.

"He says he's a businessman named Edoardo Gandini."

"How often does he come to see you?"

"Oh, I don't know—four or five times a year."

Eli leaned over and slapped the girl's face again, twice.

"That's two slaps for two lies in the last two sentences," he growled. "Now, for the last time, who came to see you tonight, and how often does he come?"

The girl started sobbing again. "I've told you. I just know him as Edoardo Gandini and he calls every two months or so."

Eli and Ran realized the girl was a tough case. She lied just for practice.

Eli whipped a vicious-looking switchblade out of his pocket and grabbed the girl's long black hair. He pulled her head back and stuck the point of the knife against her cheek. "If you don't tell me the truth in one second, I'm going to cut your face up so badly you're never going to get a call from any man again—ever. Now who is he, and when does he come here?"

The girl's eyes were bulging again with horror as she stared into Eli's stocking mask. Eli drove the point of the knife against her cheek, nicking the skin and drawing a small spot of blood.

"All right, all right," gasped the girl. "I'll tell you. He's Count Peroli and he comes every week."

The interrogation was going satisfactorily. The girl was beginning to realize the truth was best.

Eli kept the knife against her cheek. "How much does he pay you for your little services, eh?"

"Fifty," said the girl. "Fifty thousand lire. That's my standard charge. They all know that."

"Very nice, too, for you," said Eli. Ran reckoned she still had to be telling the truth. Two customers they knew about that day, and two times fifty thousand lire in her handbag.

Eli eased his grip on the girl and let her sink back

against the pillows. "And now, my little darling, what else have you been up to today?"

"Why do you want to know? What the hell business is it of yours?"

Eli jabbed the knife forward again and the girl said hastily, "Well, I did a trick with another man this afternoon, that's all—honestly it is."

"Let's leave honesty out of this after the pack of lies you've been trying to sell us," said Eli. "Now, what was the name of this other man?"

"Bergman, Johnny Bergman," said the girl quickly.

Ran—out of her line of vision—picked up the address book and flipped it over. There was the name Johnny Bergman and the words "around the first of every month" written against it. He nodded to Eli, whom he reckoned was doing very well. The ideal way of interrogating someone is never to let them know what you are really after or how much you know. So far the only thing the girl knew was that when she did tell the truth Eli kept away from her with his nasty knife. She still didn't know why they were really there.

"How long have you known Bergman?"

"Oh, about three or four years."

"And how often does he come to see you?"

"Every month," said the girl. "Around the first of every month." This was a man she didn't seem to mind telling the truth about.

"How did you meet him?"

"Well, before my guy set me up with this apartment I used to be working the street at the bottom of the via Veneto—you know the short-time hotels around there —and this fellow just walked up to me one day. When I moved off the street into the telephone side of the business I kept him on. He was a steady customer and never made any trouble."

"You mean he's not the whip and kinky boots type?"

"No, nothing like that, but he's an older guy and I have to dance around a bit to get him started up. But he's O.K. He always buys me a good lunch and it's an afternoon deal."

"Where did you have lunch today?"

"Oh, we had a great time at the Sans Souci—every drink you can think of."

The girl was sharp, and she was lying again, just to find out how much they knew. She found out the hard way as Eli leaped across the room again and ripped off her flimsy dressing gown. Eli jabbed the cold point of the knife against her right nipple, his hand over her mouth again to stifle the involuntary scream.

"It'll cost you a nipple if you don't tell me where you had lunch," said Eli. "You know the Sans Souci isn't open for lunch."

"Oh God, let me go. I forgot. It was the Eden. I swear it was the Eden."

"That's right," said Eli. "And how were the wild strawberries?"

Nice one, thought Ran. Alternate the questions to which you know the answers with the ones you don't know and let them think you know everything. Slapping whores around in Roman bedrooms was hardly what he or Eli thought they'd joined the Institute for, but Eli was doing a very professional job.

After that they could hardly stop the girl talking. With the occasional check questions on what she'd eaten for lunch, where she'd met Kent—or Wagner—or Bergman, whoever he was, the story came out. As far as she knew, he was an American. He told her he passed through Rome about once every month. He said he was in the import-export business. It was always the same routine—a call around the first of the month, a big lunch at a top restaurant and then the afternoon session. They always spoke in Italian. His was quite good, in fact good enough so that she could not be quite sure he spoke with an American accent. He said he had a wife and two children in America, but would not go into details about them when she asked, and had never gone in for that incurable American habit of flashing around pictures of his family.

Did he ever go to Germany? He told her he travelled all over Europe, spoke five languages, but she was never able to check him out on it. She spoke only two languages—Neapolitan and Italian—and couldn't even remember what languages he said he spoke.

The girl seemed to be a plain ordinary hooker. In fact, as Ran and Eli prepared to leave, she even propositioned them again. "What's with you two guys, anyway? Stay around for a while and you can get two for the price of one. You didn't have to bust in like that. Just a phone call would have done the trick. I'll bet you're cops at that."

"Maybe," said Eli. "And thanks for the offer. But we have to be going."

He peeled five ten-thousand-lire notes out of his wallet. "We'll take a rain check on it, dear. This is to pay for the man wiring up the phone again."

He ripped the phone out of the wall as he and Ran left.

He pointed to Ran who was stuffing his gun and silencer back into his pocket. "Don't tell anyone we were here or I'll send this nasty man back to have a word with you," he said as he closed the door. The pair of them clattered down the stairs.

"What do you think?" asked Ran when they got into the street.

"I think," said Eli, "that our man likes to get laid once a month—but where he gets the money I don't know."

They briefed the agent outside the house to watch the hooker until further notice.

Chapter Sixteen

Shraga "The Banker" was unhappy for three reasons as he drove the hire-car from Munich airport towards the suburb of Pasing. In the first place it was his forty-fifth birthday, one of those days when you add everything up and decide you don't like being forty-five. In the second place, forty-five was no age to be sent out on burglary jobs. And in the third place he was beginning to realize it was going to be this kind of assignment from now on until he had to settle for a minor desk job back in Israel.

He smoothed back the graying hair at his temples with one pudgy hand as he guided the car with the other and looked sideways quickly at Gabi, his assistant. The message which reached them from the Chief in Stuttgart had been short and to the point—break into Barbara Wagner's Munich home that night and look for any signs that Wagner was still alive. The brief said that Frau Wagner lived in a modest flat on Eichtinger Strasse in Munich-Pasing and apparently had had a tough time making ends meet since her husband was killed or skipped off at the end of the war. To official inquiries she had always said she had never heard from her husband, had worked for many years as a dish-washer and waitress, and was now running an evening-newspaper kiosk in the center of Munich. She usually arrived home around ten-thirty every night, and the search had to be made well before then.

Shraga and Gabi had scrambled aboard the next plane to Munich, and the afternoon was fading fast.

Shraga reckoned the speed at which they were told to do the job meant something was coming apart at the seams somewhere else, but he had no way of connecting the killing of his old friend Yehuda Katz in Rome with the possible discovery of Wagner. Before his disastrous banking venture when he was chief resident agent in Amsterdam, and demotion by previous Institute Chief Uri Haran, Shraga could have reckoned to be given a bit more information about his assignments, even though the essence of espionage work was to keep things compartmentalized. As a chief resident, though, he would have been told more, to be able to assess odds and ends of information supplied by his own men on the spot.

Now, after the banking bust-up, he was just given orders—and no explanations.

He thought back to the old days, when Uri Haran had personally come out to Buenos Aires to supervise the kidnapping of Eichmann. Privately he reckoned Haran had been a bit too panicky about the whole thing, calling meetings of the kidnap group at all hours of the day and night in different cafes and safe houses—but what the hell, there was no substitute for victory, and when Eichmann was delivered back to Israel there had been citations all around for everyone involved and whopping great bonuses. And Shraga's promotion to chief agent in Holland.

His personal friendship with Haran—and his involvement in the Eichmann coup—had just about saved his career with the Institute when they found out about his little bank on the side in Luxemburg.

Then Haran had had a big row with the then-

164

premier, David Ben Gurion, in 1963 on the political handling of the discovery that Nazi scientists were working for the Egyptian army. Ben Gurion, trying to link Israel to the "New Germany" of Konrad Adenauer, wanted to get the scientists out by secret diplomatic means. Haran, who hated everything German, deliberately leaked details of the Nazi rocket scientists to selected journalists.

When the spit hit the fan and there was uproar in Israel and Germany over the affair there was an ugly interview between Ben Gurion and Haran. Haran quit, went home to his wife Sarah and ordered her to sell her Volkswagen car a few days later as he wanted to own nothing German.

With Haran gone any chance of Shraga getting a top job again in the Institute faded too. And here he was driving along to a sneak burglary job with a trainee Institute burglar.

Gabi, twenty-five, slim and black-haired, was a complete contrast to the worldly-wise and cynical Shraga. This was to be his first break-in job for the Institute and he couldn't wait. This, he thought, was a lot more fun than finishing law school as his father had intended. But he was nervous, too.

Like all young Israelis he thought he knew better than Shraga, and map-read him around a couple of wrong turnings until Shraga leaned over and seized the road map. Gabi was continually checking his kit—two walkie-talkies, a set of keys and lock-picking equipment, two cameras with special lenses for photocopying any documents they might find lying around.

Twenty-five, he was not too sure who Barbara Wagner was, and had never heard of mass Jew-killer Colonel Heinz Wagner. To him, this was just a job.

Shraga had just grunted by way of explanation, "He's sort of another Eichmann," and let it go at that.

Bitterly he thought how short memories were. If peace ever came between Israel and the Arabs the next generation of Israelis would probably be asking one day who Nasser and Anwar Sadat were.

By this time they had reached Frau Wagner's street, Eichtinger Strasse. The small, sleazy apartment block in which she lived had three floors. Shraga had been told she had a two-room walkup on the second floor.

It was still daylight. Shraga circled the block and pulled up at a cafe. It would be lighting-up time in thirty minutes, and they could plan on starting the job half an hour after that. Shraga reckoned they would need two hours for a thorough look, and should be back out on the street at least an hour before Frau Wagner returned.

A pity the boy hadn't been doing this sort of job before, thought Shraga. Normally the break-in man would have done the whole job while the second man would keep watch outside with walkie-talkie communication.

But as the job was important, Shraga had decided he would turn the place over personally. Who knew—if he found some conclusive evidence, it could put him back on the road to favor again with the new Chief.

So Shraga went over it all again with Gabi over a coffee in the cafe. "I will stay below and keep watch while you force the door—remember, no entry marks, no one must know we have paid this little visit. When the door is ajar, down you come to take over from me and I'll go up and do the search. If there's anything that needs photographing I'll call you up over the voice-link."

Of course, for the next half-hour there was the usual argument. Young Gabi was quite sure he could do the whole job. All Shraga had to do was shamble around on the pavement outside and watch for the cops.

166

"This is what I've been trained to do," he said. "I've got to have a baptism of fire sometime."

"Yes," said Shraga, "sometime in the near future—but not tonight."

Gabi was livid and called Shraga a few choice names in Hebrew so loudly that the waiter and a couple of customers looked their way.

"You silly little sod," hissed Shraga. "You know we are never supposed to speak Hebrew in a public place."

Gabi was unrepentant. "Bugger you too—I may have to work with you but I don't have to sit here being lectured by you like some school kid. I'm going to do something useful." He stalked out of the cafe as more heads turned.

Shraga was beginning to wonder whether it might not be simpler to have a neon sign reading "Israeli burglars" on the car outside. Gabi walked off round the block and Shraga let him go, knowing an argument on the street would just attract more attention.

Gabi was back by the time it was dark. He sat down opposite Shraga again and didn't refer to their argument. "Looks pretty easy," he said. "I could see the windows and there are no lights on—looks like no one's at home. The flat's on two corners and I checked both sides."

God almighty, thought Shraga, the boy had been hanging around outside the place for about fifteen minutes. By his minimum estimation. Too late to call things off now. The job had to be done tonight.

He was too disgusted to say anything to his trainee, but planned a word in the right ears later on.

He ordered two more coffees and some sticky sweet cakes—must cut out these in-between snacks, he thought to himself as he surveyed his expanding waistline nudging the edge of the table. Another fifteen minutes and he and Gabi went out to the car. They drove several blocks away and armed themselves with their kit. Gabi put his belt stuffed with lock-picking equipment on under his jacket. Hanging down inside the jacket on one side was his camera, the walkie-talkie on the other.

Shraga just slid his walkie-talkie into an outside pocket. No guns for this job, no one was supposed to be seen or blasted. Then they rove back and parked in the street parallel to Eichtinger Strasse. Gabi mumbled once more about doing the whole job himself, and Shraga just said, "If you ever get to be in charge of an operation, which I doubt, you can make the decisions. Tonight I make them. Now let's get going."

He made Gabi walk about fifty yards ahead, saw him turn into the entranceway to the apartment block and dawdled along on the opposite side of the street. The walkie-talkie had an effective range of about a hundred yards. Shraga turned at the end of the block and walked a few steps down the side street. He wasted some more time fumbling for a cigarette and then a lighter. Then he crossed back over the intersection and walked straight back past the apartment entrance. It was blacked out, the nearest street lamp was thirty yards away and only two cars passed by. At the top of the street Shraga talked down into his jacket—it had been five minutes now—and said, "How's it going?"

On low volume, Gabi's metallic voice whispered back. "I've got problems with the lock. There may be a metal bar inside the door, but I'm working on it."

Damn youngsters, thought Shraga. When I started in this business we had fellows who could have bust into Fort Knox quicker than he's taking to get through some widow's door.

He lumbered back down the block again past the Wagner entrance. A few curtained lights in the windows around, and he could hear a television set somewhere. No one was in the street at this dinner hour. Five minutes later he checked with Gabi again.

"Still got trouble with the bar," said the boy, "but it will be all right. I need a few more minutes."

Cursing, Shraga walked back down the street again and looked up to Frau Wagner's windows.

It was then that he saw the thin pencil flash of light in one of the rooms.

Shraga turned quickly into the entranceway and, for his weight, made surprisingly little noise as he crept up to the second floor. Gabi was nowhere in sight on the small landing, but the door to the Wagner flat was slightly ajar. Shraga peered slowly around the edge of the door and saw Gabi poking around in a desk in the corner of the small living room using his pencil torch for the job.

He jumped about six feet when Shraga, sneaking right up behind him, snapped, "And just what the hell do you think you're doing?"

Gabi turned and, recovering fast, said, "I just managed to get the door open and thought I'd look around until your next call."

The bloody boy doesn't even lie convincingly, thought Shraga. He was tempted to punch him straight in the mouth for starters but this was hardly the place for a brawl. Later would be soon enough.

"Get below immediately," he said. "I told you I'd take care of this. Now get downstairs, there's no one watching either of our backs at the moment. And the first lesson you seem to have forgotten is always to pull the curtains before you fool around with torches in strange people's apartments. This place looked like a fireworks display from outside."

Chastened at last, Gabi walked to the door, managing to bump into a small table with a clatter that sounded like the Empire State building collapsing to the two burglars.

Shraga stood alone in the room, trying to fight his rage and get his bearings. He had just pulled the curtains and was checking around the room with his own torch when it happened.

In the street below a voice bellowed, "Halt, halt, halt —police," followed by three rapid shots.

Shraga's quiet little world collapsed.

There was complete pandemonium outside as Shraga leaped to the Wagner door and slammed it behind him. The hall light was switched on and he could hear window shutters clattering as people looked out into the street.

Shraga, his heart pounding, walked calmly down the steps, hoping to be able to sneak away. As he walked out of the front hallway with the light silhouetting him he had no time to see what had happened to Gabi. A searchlight suddenly stabbed into his eyes, completely blinding him, from the top of a police car as a voice shouted over a loudhailer, "Hands on your head and don't move. This is the police."

Shraga was still wondering if he could talk his way out of it—he hadn't been caught red-handed in the flat—as his hands shot to his head. The sharp movement snapped the strap underneath his jacket and his concealed walkie-talkie clattered to the ground.

Shraga looked at it in horror as two uniformed policemen lunged forward and snapped handcuffs on his wrists. Standing beside the police car, he could see a sullen Gabi, also handcuffed, as two more policemen were unloading his camera, walkie-talkie and house-busting belt.

It wasn't until the story came out in the papers that Shraga and Gabi found out there had been three burglaries in the area in the past two weeks and that an interfering old bag in one of the nearby flats had seen

Gabi on his bumbling reconnaissance and called the police when she saw him sneak in later.

And that is why Shraga didn't understand what the almost jocular police sergeant meant when he bundled them into the back of the squad car and said, "We've been looking for you lads all over the place."

Shraga knew that his only chance of getting back into the big league with the Institute had just vanished forever as he looked across silently at Gabi with an expression he usually reserved for vermin.

Chapter Seventeen

At two o'clock the next morning the scrambler telephone by the bedside of the Institute Chief rang in Tel Aviv. His wife stirred as he picked it up and listened.

After two minutes he whispered softly, "Those two stupid bastards. The only thing they're fit for is a clown act in a circus—and then only as stand-ins. Send a car right away and call in all the Section Chiefs."

He stumbled out of bed muttering under his breath and pulling clothes on as lights began to go on in office rooms all over the "Viktor Halsmann Company" real estate agents' premises on Gordon Street.

It was going to be a long, bad night.

The Chief was there in twenty minutes, as the Section Chiefs also began to arrive. Late revellers would have been surprised to see so much activity in a real estate agents' office so early in the morning.

The Chief's customary cigar was going like an old Union Pacific steam locomotive as he snatched the report from Munich out of the night duty officer's hand.

Shraga and Gabi had done the Service proud. Not only had they committed the unforgivable sin of getting caught, but the Munich police had been jumping about quite actively. As Shraga and Gabi sat silently in the police station refusing to make a statement the police had whipped around all the bars in the neighborhood

173

near Frau Wagner's flat and got a report of the argument in some strange language between two men resembling the burglars. They had got a description of the rental car and found it a block away from Eichtinger Strasse.

In Gabi's bag inside the car they found the cover identity card on which he had entered Germany. It listed him as being an Israeli Ministry of Labor employee.

It didn't take even the slow-minded Bavarian detectives long to work out why two Israelis had broken into Frau Wagner's flat especially as, when she got home, she told them that nothing was missing. The Israeli Embassy was doing its best to persuade the Munich police not to release details of the arrest, and in any case it had come too late to make the morning papers. But there was Frau Wagner, the people in the cafe and the old busybody who had reported Shraga and Gabi to the police in the first place. There was no way anyone could keep the lid on the story for more than another twenty-four hours.

The Chief thought rapidly.

The balloon man in Rome was not a great newspaper reader. The only time they had seen him buy one was yesterday morning before he met his girl friend, and then he had good reason to after the shooting of Bentor. But he had a transistor radio in his room and perhaps listened to RAI news bulletins, dreadful and uninformative as they were.

Two Israeli officials busting into the home of a Nazi war criminal's "widow" in the middle of the night was sure to make the papers and newscasts almost everywhere in Western Europe.

The balloon man looked as if he had plans to duck out already. That little item would only make him move faster. And now Israel seemed clearly involved in the whole business, as the Prime Minister had strictly forbidden. The Chief still lacked the final proof that Kent was in fact Wagner. Steiger and his marksman had already flown to Rome during the night, and he was now taking over the Kent/Wagner operation.

For a fraction of a second the Chief thought of telling Steiger to blast Kent at the first opportunity, without identifying him as Wagner, so that there would be no connection between the bungled Munich burglary and the death of an old balloon salesman in the heart of Rome.

But the Prime Minister had specifically forbidden the killing or kidnapping of the suspect without copper-bottom evidence of his real identity. If it turned out that Kent was not Wagner after Steiger's men executed him, a lot of Institute heads would roll—starting with the Chief's, particularly after the Lillehammer blunder.

If evidence came up that the balloon man was Wagner it would be quite clear, after the Munich fiasco, that it was the work of an Israeli death-squad—another P.M. veto.

The Prime Minister would have to be told of the Munich clanger early in the morning, before anyone in the Foreign Ministry went sneaking to him. That gave the Chief about five or six hours to come up with something new.

He gulped hot coffee and ordered about a gallon more for the meeting with the Section Chiefs, then summoned them to his office.

There was a gloomy silence when he had finished his briefing and added the bit about the institution's hands being tied by the Prime Minister.

"The truth of the matter is," said the Chief, "that if, as we have every reason to believe, Kent is Wagner and skips out of Italy we will lose him if he runs to an Arab country like Libya. Our problem is to make sure he cannot leave Italy without directly involving the State

175

of Israel."

In the next hour and a half, as the first light of dawn began to stab the Israeli sky, a lot of coffee was drunk and the Section Chiefs came up with some weird ideas. The Chief listened, his head disappearing from time to time in a fog of cigar smoke.

The clearest idea was that if the Israelis were not allowed to grab Kent now, the only other people who could were the Italians, despite the efforts that had been made so far to keep them out of the whole business. Up till now everyone had agreed that if the Italians were persuaded to arrest Kent there was a great risk that Arabs or Fascist elements in the country, and within the police force itself, might quietly let him go.

But Kent in the hands of the Italians was about a thousand per cent better than Kent in the hands of the Libyans. And the Israelis did have at least a couple of friends in the Italian Interior Ministry and the various police departments.

The major problem was how to get Kent denounced.

If the State of Israel demanded Kent's extradition for crimes against the Jewish people, there would be an immediate furor in Italy. People would be jumping around trying to protect him. The Italian Government would do almost anything to avoid making a decision, and anxious to preserve relations with the Arabs whose oil they so badly needed, would go to almost any lengths to avoid sending him to Israel.

At this stage the least possible Israeli involvement was paramount.

As the Chief pointed out, "It doesn't necessarily have to be an Israeli or even a Jew who denounces him. Wagner did one helluva job on the Jews, but his tastes were fairly catholic. Plenty of French, Russians, Poles and even Germans passed through his hands. Any one of them would be delighted to take the credit for turn-

176

ing him in. And if he is denounced by a non-Jewish source, that will leave our hands free for dealing with him later if our initial involvement is sufficiently blurred. Plenty of Gentiles would like to pull the trigger on him."

With the principle of denunciation decided, the Chief and his men worked through the list of Nazi-hunting organizations. There were people like Simon Wiesenthal in Vienna, several organizations inside Germany itself, the International Concentration Camps Committee in Paris, and the Brussels-based International Resistance and Deportation Union led by a non-Jew, Hubert Mercier.

They finally settled on the International Justice and Deportees Association, headquartered in Paris.

The I.J.D.A. was headed by a Gentile Frenchman, Paul Baurdoux, and had mostly non-Jewish members. But Baurdoux was a good friend of the Israelis, and plenty of information about Nazi war criminals had been exchanged in the past.

To keep Israel even further out of the denunciation, the Chief decided that Baurdoux should be given most of the details of the Kent/Wagner dossier to date, omitting the reference to the murder of Bentor, which the Israelis could handle in their own way later. Baurdoux would be asked to denounce Kent to the Germans.

Bonn in turn would be obliged to make an official complaint to the Italians and demand Kent's extradition.

The Italians would listen more kindly to a German extradition request and would probably be only too glad to get rid of a hot potato. With luck, Israel's name could be kept reasonably in the background during the hubbub, and if something unpleasant happened to Wagner later, no one would be able to point a finger directly at Tel Aviv.

"There remains the problem of these two blithering idiots in Munich—Shraga and Gabi—who've got Israel written all over them," said the Chief. Looking at the Chief of the German Section, he said, "You will have to get a message to them. They cannot deny they are Israelis now, but it is essential that they should say they were a pair of amateurs—they behaved like it anyway—and that they happened to be in Munich and thought of looking around the Wagner woman's house on the off chance of finding something. Give them a relative or two each who were killed in one of the Wagner camps. It's not good, but it's the best we can do at the moment."

As an after thought he added, "The best thing they can do is plead guilty and keep the trial as short and unsensational as possible. That way they may only have to do a couple of months, but"—looking through a billowing smoke ring with a snarl—"if the judge throws the key away on them, it's O.K. by me."

The meeting broke up as the Section Heads raced off to brief Paris and Germany.

The Chief himself sent all the bad news to Steiger in Rome.

There was someone else he had to break it to, too.

The Chief looked at his watch. It was seven-thirty.

He sighed and buzzed his secretary. "Tell the P.M.'s office I need an urgent appointment, and cancel any meetings not concerning the Kent operation for the rest of the day, dear. And bring me lots more coffee."

Chapter Eighteen

By eleven o'clock in the morning the Chief's painful interview with the Prime Minister was over.

"Well, Chief," he had said, "all this seems to be getting very complicated. One or two things seem to be going wrong."

On the Chief's new plan to have Kent denounced, the P.M. had carefully rowed back out of the line of fire. "As the State is hopefully now being kept out of this— provided there are no more mistakes—I hope it all works out well for you. Keep me closely informed."

You had to hand it to the Old Man, thought the Chief, he was all politician. He had rubber-stamped the Institute project, but made it clear who was responsible.

A carefully doctored Kent/Wagner file had already been sent on the early El Al flight to Paris and was now being picked up at Orly airport. The Institute agent in Paris was in the I.J.D.A. Office on the rue des Beaux-Arts by midday closeted with Paul Baurdoux, with handsome blow-ups of the Kent photographs, file pictures of Wagner, the handwriting samples and the fingerprints, just for laughs, because no one seemed to have any of Wagner's war-time prints around.

Baurdoux, a thin, white-haired man with a permanent limp from the beatings he had taken in Buchenwald, looked over the file and said to the agent, "This looks pretty good. But why are you telling me all this? Why don't you hand it to the Germans yourself?"

The agent patted him on the shoulder. "Listen, Paul, you know we've worked together in the past. I don't quite know the answer myself. They didn't give me the full picture. It looks as if we don't want to be mixed up in it directly and thought it would look nicer coming from you. I think there will be something on the news wires today, and that is what I really wanted to talk to you about. I think we want you to tell a small fib to the Germans."

By one o'clock it had happened. Agence France-Presse came up with a brief dispatch from Munich saying that two Israelis had been arrested the night before and had been charged with attempting to burglarize Frau Wagner's flat.

The Institute agent came back to see his friend Baurdoux with the piece of agency tape.

"The small fib, *mon ami*, is this. We want you to tell the Germans that your people had been working on the file we have given you, that it comes from your organization, not ours. And that because you have just seen the news of the attempted burglary in Munich you think it may alert the man in Rome and cause him to flee. That is why you are denouncing him now—*tu comprends*?"

Baurdoux looked at the piece from Munich and nodded slowly.

"I think I'm beginning to get the message. I should imagine the chances of early promotion for your two burglars are quite bleak," he observed dryly.

"I wouldn't put it that way," the agent grinned. "Let's just say they're going to have to break a few world records for the hundred-yard dash just to avoid being demoted lower than office cleaners."

"When do you want me to contact the Germans?"

asked Baurdoux.

"No hurry," said the agent, picking up Baurdoux's telephone receiver. "How about right now?"

Within six hours Baurdoux had landed at Berlin's Tempelhof airport and was in the office of the Public Prosecutor in charge of the files on the R.S.H.A., Hitler's umbrella organization which controlled the Gestapo, the German Criminal Investigation Department (KRIPO) and the Sicherheitsdienst—the SS Security and Espionage Service. It had had Himmler as its overlord, with charmers like Heinrich Mueller, Eichmann and Wagner as the choirboys.

The Public Prosecutor's men were fascinated by Baurdoux's dossier. They ran around and produced their own files on Wagner, matching up wartime pictures with those taken of Kent in Rome. They all agreed the similarity was striking. Baurdoux was taken to see the assistant Prosecutor in charge of the Wagner case, officially handed over his file (he had duplicates of everything) and swore out a formal complaint alleging Kent and Wagner were the same man.

Baurdoux told the tale of his alarm at the arrest of the two Israelis in Munich very well, and impressed the need for speed on the Germans.

"Herr Baurdoux," said the assistant Prosecutor, "I can assure you we take your information and documents very seriously indeed and we shall act upon them immediately. Our car will take you to your hotel."

As Baurdoux left, the assistant Prosecutor looked up at the young examining magistrate, Peter Wendland, who had helped take the Frenchman's deposition and said, "I really do think he is on to something. You must go to Munich immediately and confront Frau Wagner with these photographs. Get out a list of addresses of all the other close associates of Wagner. We will send copies of the photographs to them, too, to see what they think. We will have to be very quick about all this, as the man in Rome may become alarmed by that Munich burglary and run for it.

"I need hardly add that the utmost discretion is imperative. Do not get the Munich detectives involved in this. Go straight to Frau Wagner at whatever time in the night you arrive. I want to get the necessary papers over to Bonn first thing in the morning if this thing holds up."

The young magistrate was practically running out of the office by the time the assistant Prosecutor had finished. A virulent anti-Nazi, born several years after the end of the war, he would do a conscientious job.

Only seven people in the Public Prosecutor's office knew why Baurdoux had arrived so hastily.

When he left the office that evening, the assistant Prosecutor called a number in Pullach, headquarters of the Bundesnachrichtendienst, the West German Federal Intelligence Service which succeeded the postwar intelligence setup of General Reinhard Gehlen. It took about twenty minutes for the BND's chief agent in Rome to get a message telling him to slap a watch on the balloon man in the Piazza Navona.

That meant that now the spooks of three nations — Israel, West Germany and Britain—all knew about Kent.

By eleven o'clock the same evening Magistrate Wendland was hammering on the door of Frau Wagner's flat in Eichtinger Strasse. A dumpy gray-haired, tired-looking woman opened it and said, "Haven't you reporters any mercy? I know nothing more than I said this morning. These men broke in and stole nothing. I don't know why."

She looked startled when he introduced himself, and

grudgingly invited him in.

Wendland laid out a dozen photographs taken of Kent in Rome on her dining table. "Do you know this man?" he asked her.

Frau Wagner looked, and sat down abruptly. Wendland thought for a moment she was going to pass out.

She said faintly, "My God—it's him."

Wendland felt a tingling excitement as he put the question formally, "Frau Wagner, are you sure you can identify these photographs as being of your husband, SS Colonel Heinz Wagner?"

"Oh yes," she said. "Now he looks the image of his father when he died, seven years ago."

Wendland left his card and told Frau Wagner to advise his office by telephone if she moved away from home. Then he ran downstairs and dialed the assistant Prosecutor in Berlin with the news.

The German Prosecutor's office had already acted fast. As Wendland was flying to Munich, another special courier had flown to the Foreign Ministry in Bonn.

By midnight the Foreign Ministry had sent an urgent telex to the Italian Foreign Ministry asking that Kent be detained immediately until identification formalities could be completed—and informing them that the full dossier would be arriving during the day, with a formal extradition request.

The ball was now in the Italians' court. Kent should have been arrested during the night.

In the event, the Italians fumbled the ball with their customary alacrity, and the telex did not reach the right office at the Rome Questura until ten in the morning. As far as the Italians were concerned, if Kent had read about the Wagner apartment break-in attempt in Munich in the Italian morning papers, he could have been on his way to Timbuctoo before the police even started looking for him.

Chapter Nineteen

On the evening Shraga and Gabi were arrested in Munich, Steiger dashed home to Bat Yam to pick up the case that was permanently parked there. It had none of the James Bond characteristics, it didn't explode if you opened it the wrong way and there were no guns inside it—but it was a special case just the same. The leather foldover grip had been made in Italy, the shirts and underwear were from Harrods and there were a couple of lightweight suits from Simpsons.

Nothing had been made in Israel.

For his flight to Rome, Steiger was to travel as a businessman on a South African passport. He and the marksman Avi were flying via Athens and when they changed planes in Greece there would be no trace that they had come from Israel. At Rome airport the brief police form the two men handed in would say they had come from Athens and all they had to remember to do was burn the ticket stubs from Tel Aviv to Athens while they were flying the Athens-Rome portion of the journey.

To his wife Mary, Steiger said, "I have to go away again for awhile."

It would be his first trip out of the country since he had been shot in Paris.

Mary looked worried, but she knew better than to

ask where he was going. "Do you know if it will be a long time, dear?"

"Don't think so," mumbled Steiger, giving her a big bearhug. "I promise we'll go away together soon on a real holiday. The office will keep in touch with you."

From the window she watched his car disappear up the road back into Tel Aviv.

Steiger went back to headquarters and heaved the bag as if it were a cigarette pack onto the table in the search room. Steiger knew his business, but the two searchers emptied out the bag anyway and checked every item. Then they gave him a thorough personal search. As a matter of habit Steiger smoked American cigarettes, and automatically, every time he bought a pack in Israel at an atrocious price, he tore off the Israeli tax stamp on the top.

He never used matches, just a battered old Ronson lighter fifteen years old.

So the searchers didn't even have to take away his smoking materials.

As a matter of routine, too, Steiger and Avi both watched carefully as their bags were searched at Tel Aviv's Ben Gurion airport. The girls doing the job asked both men if they had been to any of the Arab areas occupied by Israel in the past few days and if anyone had asked them to take a package to a friend outside Israel. The girl searching Steiger peered into the back of his Japanese camera, took the battery out of his small transistor radio after switching it on and packed it separately. She even squirted a short burst out of his aerosol shaving-cream can.

An American woman tourist standing at the bench beside him was complaining loudly as the girl searcher insisted on sending her hair drier off for testing.

It took about two hours to check all the passengers through security. Steiger thought back to the good old days when you could skid into an airport on your ear twenty minutes before flight time and they would still shove you on board.

The flight from Athens to Rome was in the dark and there was nothing to see. Steiger and Avi both slept all the way. They had both learned long ago to grab sleep whenever possible. Sniper Avi was no beady-eyed youngster. At forty-eight he was gaining weight and had a bit of a rheumatism problem. A former member of the Israeli International Olympics shooting team, he had been called up during the War of Attrition decreed by Nasser across the Suez Canal following the Six-Day War. With his night-sight, patiently waiting in his hideout near the top of one of the bunkers—overrun later in the Yom Kippur War—he had made six notches in the old Mauser rifle he favored. It was during the long cold desert nights that he noticed his rheumatism was getting worse.

At Rome's Fiumicino airport it took forty-five minutes for the two men's baggage to come through. It always does, even when there's no strike on.

This time the unloaders had added an extra little twist to the frustration of one of the world's most inefficient airports. As passengers waited for their bags at Bay 7 as the electronic signboard had instructed them, the bags were carefully pumped through Bay 3. It took another fifteen minutes to find out about that—and a lot of shouting at baggage clerks.

Steiger was ready to strangle everyone when they finally climbed into a taxi for the fifteen-mile drive to Rome. But he had to admit that the Italians were artistic bastards. The floodlighting of the Colosseum and the Arch of Constantine as they passed the Forum was magnificent. There were soft lights, too, at the far end of the Forum on the Arch of Titus, where Steiger and the Chief had decided Wagner's body was to be dumped.

Steiger told the cab driver to put them off at the gaudy, Mussolini-marbled central railway station in the heart of Rome. They bought two tickets on the next suburban train leaving town and waited in the carriage by the door. As the guard signalled for the train to start, Steiger and Avi bustled off with their bags as it started pulling out. No one else jumped off the train.

Then they took a cab around to the Bellini Travel Service off the via Bissolati. By the time they got there, Shraga and Gabi had just been arrested in Munich.

Steiger had called a meeting of all the senior operatives on the Kent/Wagner assignment—Ran, Eli, Shlomo—and he'd also asked Zipporah to come along. His idea was that Zipporah, still shocked at the murder of her lover, should be heavily involved in the whole operation, rather like a pilot who crashes a plane and is immediately ordered aloft again.

At the meeting in the back room of the Bellini Travel Service he said quietly to the unsmiling girl, "I'm sorry, Zipporah, there's not much else I can say. Except that you know we won't let this man get away with it." She just nodded and leaned back in her chair. The eyes of the four men in the room locked on to her curves like laser beams.

It was the first time Ran had seen her since she had left his bed two days before, but there was no chance to talk to her privately now.

Can't be long before someone takes her mind off Yossi, thought Steiger, little knowing that Ran had tried his best.

He slapped Ran on the back with a gigantic palm—a lesser man would have been knocked flat on his face—and boomed, "So it seems you're getting a bit more interested in these old Nazis now, eh?"

Then he got down to business. First he heard the

three men report that Kent had emerged at the usual time that day and started selling his balloons again in the usual way. He had done nothing unusual except to have lunch in a local trattoria before going to the Piazza Navona.

"I calculate that he still has some of the money he drew yesterday," said Ran.

The four men and the girl smoked and drank coffee for another two hours, going over the operation so far and the handicap the Israeli Prime Minister had given them. During the meeting they got a call to say that Kent had gone back to his attic in the usual way. He seemed to be settling back into a routine pattern.

"Or," said Steiger, "he's just trying to lull anyone watching him."

When the meeting broke up, Steiger took Ran as his second in command off for a drink at Rosati's on the Piazza del Popolo as the late Roman crowd wandered by in the warm night air. They wasted time over Scotch and sodas discussing their next moves. The conversation became academic because Steiger checked into a small hotel near the Piazza Colonna and seemed to have been asleep only a few minutes before the Bellini Travel Service called. It was, in fact, six o'clock in the morning Rome time, and the message from the Chief had come through telling Steiger that Shraga and Gabi had goofed, and Kent was being denounced that day.

Shit, thought Steiger, where do we go from here?

He summoned everyone to the Travel Service office again and broke the news.

There was nothing they could do until the Italian police came along and arrested Kent.

At the British Embassy Keane said to Burke, "I really can't figure out what the hell's going on, Joe. Kent

189

suddenly changes his pattern the day before yesterday, gets hold of some money from God knows where, spends the day on a bender with some Italian broad and then goes straight back to his hovel. Yesterday he goes back to selling balloons as if nothing had happened. We know the Israelis went up and had a word with the bird later, but we haven't had a go at her ourselves as you told me just to keep an eye on things. The Israelis are still watching her too, but as far as we can make out she's just a straight call girl."

"I'm afraid we'll just have to keep watching it," said Burke. "The Israelis still obviously think he's Wagner and he killed their boy, and they're not going to let go until they've sorted it out. They may be right about him being Wagner, at that. From what you tell me they have eight people working on this thing—and God knows how many we haven't spotted yet. Anyway, what about a spot of lunch?"

He looked at his watch as he stood up. It was ten past one.

As he and Keane made for the door, Burke's secretary came in and said, "They thought you ought to see this right away."

It was a couple of paragraphs on Reuter saying that two men identified as Israelis had been found attempting to burgle Frau Wagner's Munich flat the night before.

"Ho ho ho," sniggered Burke. "Looks like the Israelis have made a right balls-up. I wonder how they'll get out of that one?"

Chapter Twenty

Anyone monitoring the volume of Israeli coded traffic that day would have noticed a sharp rise in volume between Tel Aviv, Paris, Berlin, Munich and Rome as all the moves in the denunciation of the man believed to be Wagner were passed around.

Steiger pulled every available man and woman in on the job. He had double watches put on Kent and his momentary girl friend —his only other known contact with the outside world—and he staked out the Piazza Navona and every exit from it, with four back-up cars and drivers.

Steiger assumed the Italian police would calculate that a man like Kent, if he really was Wagner, might walk around armed. But in case Kent managed to shoot his way out of it, Steiger had no intention of letting him get away from the Institute. He would then be a man on the run and Steiger's boys were going to keep running right alongside him.

He ran the operation from the Travel Office and told Ran, in charge of the men on the spot, to call him every hour on the hour, even if nothing unusual was happening.

"What I mean is," he boomed, "I want a call from you even if he farts. Got it?"

Over lunch, Burke and Keane worked out that the

Israelis were likely to make a desperate move in Rome after the arrest of their Munich burglars and decided to double the British watch too, adding a couple of photographers.

"You never know your luck," chortled Burke. "If the Institute decides to pinch Kent we might get the whole sequence on film."

The prospect of inviting a few Israeli "diplomats" around to watch some "artistic shots in the streets of historic Rome" tickled him enormously.

That day Kent shuffled downstairs from his attic at about one o'clock and around to the corner restaurant. There were chairs and tables outside in the hot sun, and the Israeli men noted approvingly that Kent, still presumably using the money he had got from the bank, ordered a plain bowl of spaghetti with butter and grated parmesan cheese without tomato or meat sauce. He followed that up with boiled beef and potatoes.

Wagner was a man who was supposed to like plain boiled food.

The bender with the Italian whore at the roof restaurant of the Eden was clearly the exception that proved the rule.

Clutching his leather pouch after lunch, Kent wandered back to his attic. He stared briefly at the newsstand on the corner but didn't buy a newspaper. There would not have been time to catch the early afternoon editions anyway with the report from Munich of Shraga and Gabi's arrests.

Kent came downstairs again at about three. This time he had his hydrogen can and balloon equipment with him, the little trestle table and the pouch tucked under his arm. He gave his customary nervous glance each way up the street before stepping out of the doorway and heading onto the Piazza Navona. It was the best time of day to be in the Square. The sun shimmered down and the water of the three fountains glistened. In the canvas-topped enclosures outside the square's four or five restaurants, late lunchers were clinking coffee spoons. But every respectable Italian was already home bashing his ear for the inviolable afternoon siesta. In Rome, those two hours are the quietest of the day or night.

The balloon man sat on a stone bench opposite the Tre Scalini cafe and prepared all his kit for the day's business. Things were slow at that hour. He didn't sell a balloon for forty-five minutes.

And in that time five Institute and three British agents, spread out in four coffee shops round the Piazza, had drunk a total of eighteen coffees, costing their respective services almost two and a half pounds.

As the Piazza began to fill again in the late afternoon with hippies, lovers, tourists and strollers, Kent's business began to pick up.

On his routine seven o'clock call to Steiger, Ran heard that the Germans had now been told about Kent in Berlin and had promised to treat the matter urgently.

Ran quietly sidled round the square and its approaches, telling his group not to blink from now on.

On the nine o'clock call that night Ran told Steiger: "I think we've got company. The guy watching Kent's place says a BMW with a couple of men drove past twice half an hour ago. It's not the kind of street for that sort of car. They parked up the far end and then walked past Kent's doorway and stopped to light cigarettes near it. Now they've gone down to the Tre Scalini cafe and are watching Kent."

Steiger frowned. "What number plate have they got?"

"Roman," said Ran, and read it to him. "But they're speaking German at the cafe."

Damn, thought Steiger. The Krauts were on to it

within three hours of being told. But which Krauts were they? If they were from the Gehlen mob that wasn't so bad. The BND were allowed to take an interest—although he made a note for future checking to find out who the informant was in the Berlin Public Prosecutor's Office. But suppose the source at the Prosecutor's Office had told one of the Nazi underground groups, who made it their business to tip off former colleagues in danger?

To Ran he said, "They are probably from the BND. If they were the bad guys they wouldn't just be sitting around watching. They would have approached Kent and told him to clear off as fast as possible. But I'm sending an extra man down now just to watch them."

At this stage a dozen foreign secret service men were milling around the Piazza. The British knew the Israelis were there, the Israelis knew some kind of Germans were there, the Germans knew Kent was there, and Kent knew nothing at all.

At eleven o'clock that night Ran reported that Kent was beginning to get his gear together and seemed about to go home. Steiger still had no definite information from Tel Aviv that the Italian police had been officially asked to arrest him. It looked as if it were going to be the midnight knock at Kent's room.

Ran hung the phone up in the Tre Scalini and walked quickly up the road to the corner of the via di Parione, two blocks away from the square, past which Kent always walked on his way home. Two other men were marking the Germans, who had not moved from the cafe. And two more were to follow Kent out of the square past Ran. Eli was sitting in a car twenty feet from Ran as he lolled on the street corner. The lights were out and the engine was idling.

Kent, carrying his trestle, cylinder and pouch walked up the via Sant'Agnese in Agone, over the intersection

194

just beyond which Yossi Bentor had been shot down, and headed the fifty yards up the street towards Ran. Near the little cafe where Kent had eaten lunch earlier in the day, two young men were fiddling with a motor scooter whose engine was running.

Kent shuffled past them. He had made about ten paces when the two Italians jumped on the scooter and roared off behind him. Kent half turned as the scooter bore down on him and stepped sideways at the same as the Italian riding pillion reached out and grabbed the leather pouch from under Kent's arm. The impact knocked Kent against the wall and he fell in a heap, his hydrogen cylinder and trestle table clattering around him.

The scooter belted up the street toward Ran. He was the only obstacle between the pouch thieves and a clean getaway.

In a split second Ran realized that he and Eli could never catch them in a car through the narrow streets behind the Piazza. And he realized, too, that, whoever had grabbed the pouch, it was the one thing the Institute had to have.

The orders had been not to alarm Kent in any way. But someone had just done that anyway.

Ran was standing in the shadows as the scooter hurtled towards him. He thought of the gun under his shoulder. With the light behind the two riders, they presented a perfect target.

But Ran had to know who these people were.

This was what all his training and his years as a reserve paratrooper were about. Ran braced himself low against the wall as the scooter bore down. The getaway route seemed to be along the via di Parione as the driver was coming closer to the wall on Ran's side. Ran aimed off for deflection and rammed himself away from the wall, feet together and parallel to the ground, like a wrestler bounding off the ropes towards his opponent.

The aim was perfect.

Both his feet crashed into the side of the driver's head, snapping it sideways and backwards. The driver fell back and the scooter reared up like a prancing horse, the throttle racing crazily as he ripped it wide open in his agony. Ran was spun around in mid-air by the impact, but he landed like a cat as the scooter careened on past him. Instead of turning the corner, it crashed into the storefront opposite with a horrendous shattering of glass. The scooter bounced back and both riders were dashed to the ground. The pillion passenger landed six feet away spread-eagled on his back. The driver landed under the scooter, whose rear wheel was still racing wildly.

Ran made a crouching turn and his Beretta with its silencer was already in his hand as he surveyed the scene. Near the pillion rider's outstretched arm lay Kent's leather pouch.

The reaction of the average man in the street to a sudden event is extraordinarily long. It takes about five seconds for a man to hear the screeching of brakes, an impact, perhaps a cry, before he has realized what has happened, and where, before he even starts to make a decision about what his next action will be.

It also takes five seconds for a sprinter to run fifty yards.

In this case Ran was the sprinter, and everyone else was the man in the street. Ran knew he needed that pouch and he also knew he needed to know why two young men on a motor scooter thought fit to swipe it.

People in the corner cafe were only just beginning to fight their way out the door as Ran bounded over and seized the pouch. He looked quickly at the scooter driver, who was lying under the scooter but not screaming. He was dead or unconscious.

But the pillion passenger, the man who had grabbed Kent's pouch in the first place, had his eyes wide open and was trying to get up. Ran shoved his pistol right under the boy's nose and yelled *"Avanti, presto!"* tugging at his hair. He heard a whimper start from the boy's mouth as he yanked him to his feet.

Ran looked around. Eli was standing at the door of the car. Ran hurled the leather pouch at Eli and gave the pillion rider a brutal shove in the back. Eli grabbed the pouch, tossed it into the car and ripped the rear door open. In another four seconds, Ran had crammed his prisoner into the back seat, jumped in beside him, and was slamming the door was Eli accelerated away.

Eli didn't have his number plate lights on anyway, and none of the ten people who ran out of the cafe could later tell the police for sure the number or make of the getaway car.

Eli careened down the via di Parione and two more side streets before he got out onto the Corso Vittorio Emmanuele and turned right over the Tiber. In the back seat Ran looked over his victim, who was whining, "I give up, I surrender."

He had blood running from his nose, a cut on his forehead and a lot of abrasions on his back and the back of his head. But from the amount of noise he was making, it seemed as if he would live.

Somehow Ran seemed to have ripped a hole in the calf of his trouser leg, and he could feel blood trickling down. But he reckoned he would live too.

On the other side of the river Eli turned off before the Vatican and coasted up the slope leading to the Janiculum Gardens, the haunt of courting couples in cars and people who want to have a private chat. He drove past the statue of Garibaldi at the top of the gardens and stopped in a side alleyway among the trees.

Then he turned and looked at his passengers.

"You O.K.?" he asked Ran.

Ran nodded and they both looked at the prisoner. Ran still had his pistol jammed under the boy's ear—he looked as if he were about nineteen—and he was staring at them in terror, moaning more from fear than from pain.

He looked up at the two men and whined, "All right, I snatched the old guy's pouch. Why don't we go down to the station? Look, I'm bleeding. I need a doctor."

Eli leaned over to the backseat and said benignly in Italian, "O.K., little fella, we'll get you a doctor any time now. Just a couple of questions first. Who told you to slap the old guy and take his pouch?"

The youth's eyes widened. "Whatcha mean, mister? Me and my buddy figured it all out by ourselves. We seen he takes in a bit of scratch selling those crazy balloons. We've been on the snatch game down in Trastevere and thought we'd move it over the river. That old guy takes six, maybe seven thousand lire a night." The boy's nose was beginning to pour blood. He crammed a handkerchief against it and looked horrified when he saw the crimson stain.

"Please, officers, can I please see a doctor now?"

Eli looked at Ran.

"We'll have to take him in," said Ran in English. "It sounds genuine, but we have to be sure they weren't put up to this."

As Eli drove slowly back into Rome, Ran looked into the pouch. In the darkened back of the car he could see that the gun was still there.

At the via di Parione all attention was focused on the white-faced youth lying silently under his motor scooter. None of the Italians seemed to have seen the incident in which Kent's bag was snatched.

The balloon man picked himself up painfully and

collected his trestle and hydrogen cylinder. He knew the leather pouch had gone, along with his gun.

He walked slowly up the street to the point where people were crowded around the fallen scooter, but he did not even pause as he made his way home. Only the German, British and Israeli agents who had watched the whole incident knew that Kent had seen Ran grab his bag—and that, for some reason, he wasn't prepared to make trouble about it.

Chapter Twenty-One

Ran limped into the back room at the Bellini Travel Service clutching Kent's pouch. Steiger and Zipporah jumped up as they saw his torn jacket sleeve and the blood coming from his trouser leg.

"Christ, man," said Steiger in his thick South African accent—an unlikely expression for a Jew—"have we been waiting to hear from you! Shlomo called us up and told us what had happened. Are you badly hurt?"

Ran looked down at his leg, which was beginning to feel stiff and painful. "I don't think so. Must have been scraped worse than I thought when the scooter went by. How's the scooter driver?"

"He's alive," said Steiger. "But he's not feeling so good. God knows what the Italian doctors will do to him."

"Eli's in the car with the other young lout," said Ran. "Looks like it was a straight coincidence they went for him on a routine bag-snatching job—there are three dozen a night in this town. But we kept hold of him, just in case. He needs a doctor pretty quickly. He's bleeding all over the back seat."

"That's all right," said Steiger. "We've got the doc laid on and waiting. Maybe he'd better take a look at you, too."

Ran looked at the gash in his leg again. "No," he

said. "I'll stick with it if you've got some first aid stuff here."

Zipporah hurried out to send Eli off to the doctor with the young thief and came back with swabs and bandages. As she worked on Ran's leg, Steiger said, "The cat's really out of the bag now, but you did the only thing possible. We had to get that pouch. Now let's have a look in it."

Gingerly they opened up the bag. Steiger lifted out the black-metalled Smith and Wesson .38 by the barrel with a handkerchief. It was fully loaded in all six chambers. Then there was the box of ammunition, also full. Wrapped in a piece of newspaper were a separate cleaning rod, some pull-through and a phial of cleaning oil. Steiger carefully swung out the cylinder and peered down the barrel. The rifling was spotless and the revolver was clearly kept in tip-top condition.

"No way of telling if it was fired recently," he muttered. "But it was certainly cleaned not long ago."

The two men looked back in the pouch. It contained a bundle of papers held together with a clip.

The top document was a dog-eared letter dated eighteen months ago and addressed to Herr Alfred H. Kent, Poste Restante, Piazza San Silvestro, 00187 Roma, Italien. It was from the Head Office of the Swiss Bank Corporation at 6 Paradeplatz in Zurich.

It read, in English, "Dear Mr. Kent: Following your permanent written instruction this is to confirm that the amount accruing from interest on the fiduciary account held by you with us is no longer to be sent to the Banca Commerciale on the first of every month, but should in future be transmitted to the Banco della Mercede, via del Corso branch. In reply to your further question the current interest is at the rate of 10% per annum. We further confirm receiving your order that all correspondence in connection with this account should be held in our files until further notice."

It was initialed by a sub-manager.

"Well, well, well, now isn't that something," grunted Steiger. "Our chum has got himself a little numbered account in Switzerland."

He grabbed a pen and notepad and started scribbling. "He drew the equivalent of eighty pounds at the bank the other day. That means he's getting twelve times that every year, about nine hundred and sixty pounds. And if the interest rates are still about the same that means Kent has nearly ten thousand pounds stashed away in Zurich."

It wasn't the big football win, but it wasn't the kind of money you get together from selling balloons, either.

The documents under the letter from Zurich made Steiger's and Ran's eyes open even wider.

There was a piece of headed notepaper certifying that the holder, Alfred Kent, was entitled to access to the safe-deposit vault of the Banco della Mercede where he was renting safe-deposit box No. 84682. It specified that the holder must produce the present document, some form of identity card bearing a photograph and must on each occasion on which he wished to examine his box sign a special request form in the presence of the safe-deposit guard.

They looked back in the pouch.

"There it is," breathed Steiger. Taped to the side of the pouch and glistening under the lamp wa the last item.

A silver double-sided key with the number 84682 carved on it.

The last document was a Foreigner's Residence Permit bearing one of those unrecognizable Photomaton photographs made out for Alfred Herbert Kent, issued in 1958.

The I.D. Card said that Kent was born in 1906 at

Wichita Falls, Texas, was living in the via Alessandro Poerio and was employed at the American Express Company in the Piazza di Spagna. It said that Kent was permitted to stay in Italy "for the duration of his employment."

As Steiger and Ran stared at the articles on the desk, the telephone rang. Steiger listened for a few moments and said, "Keep right after him. We mustn't lose him now."

He hung up and said to Ran and Zipporah, "That was Shlomo. He says Kent has taken off. He went back to his attic, changed into that crazy suit and hat again, and has just stepped back onto the street. He's walking across Rome and seems to be very worried. He looks back at each corner and keeps doing his usual act of suddenly crossing the street without any reason. He is a very worried guy.

"Shlomo says those Krauts that were watching the house were fooled by the getup and didn't see him go. It looks as if this may be the big getaway."

It was one o'clock in the morning.

Ran and Steiger analyzed the documents they had found.

"Now we've got a man that looks like Wagner, has a Swiss bank account, a safe-deposit box here and a gun. He is the prime suspect for killing Yossi. He's so scared he doesn't run to the police when his gun and personal papers are stolen. In fact, it looks as if he's making a break," summed up Steiger. "On the other hand he has an identity card from the Italian police listing him as an American. That means he must have produced some satisfactory identification to the Italian police way back in 1958."

Ran rubbed his sore leg. "To me, the I.D. Card doesn't prove he's not Wagner. The Nazis must have spent a lot of time when they saw which way the war

203

was going preparing foolproof cover identities. Wagner was the shadow of the Gestapo Chief Heinrich Mueller. You can bet your last kopek both of them prepared new papers for years ahead. Maybe Wagner is now preparing to drop the Kent cover and has just decided to disappear and re-emerge as someone else later."

Steiger stubbed another cigarette on the pile of butts he'd already smoked that day and night.

"There's a couple of things we can start checking on right away."

He called in Avi, the marksman, who was also their weapons expert.

"Avi, we need this test-fired for a ballistics check. You'd better fire off about six rounds, as we may have to let the gun go and we'll want a couple of duplicates."

Avi disappeared, holding the revolver carefully in his handkerchief, to a cellar below the Travel Office where several bales of cotton wadding had been prepared days ago, precisely in case the Institute managed to get Kent's firearm.

Steiger started drafting an urgent cable to Tel Aviv to tell them what had happened and to ask them to check whether a man called Kent had been born in Wichita Falls in 1906.

He also made arrangements for a forgery expert to start working on the Kent signature and fixing the photograph on the Italian Residence Permit.

"I'd give a lot to see what's in that safe deposit box," said Steiger. "Who knows—maybe I will."

The reports of Kent's movements were coming in half-hourly now.

And they were coming in to an office at the British Embassy, too, where Burke and Keane were punishing the office bottle and sitting in a haze of smoke.

At the Italian Foreign Ministry, a night clerk had already received the urgent German request for Kent's arrest and left it on the Duty Officer's desk. The Duty Officer was at the apartment of his mistress after an excellent dinner and didn't call in to check for messages until six o'clock in the morning.

Well before that time, Kent had zigzagged his way from the Piazza Navona to the Piazza San Silvestro, where the main post office has an all-night telex and telephone office. It was two hundred yards from the flat where he had spent three hours with the call girl Angela Di Pozzo.

He dropped a slug in the call box and dialed a seven-digit number.

It's a local number, thought Shlomo, standing at the next booth.

He heard Kent say after a few seconds, "Hallo, Angela, it's Johnny—yes, Johnny Bergman. I stayed in town longer than I expected. How about me coming up and seeing you right now?. . . What's that?. . . Asking about me?" There was a longer pause. Then, in a whisper, "Did you say two of them with guns? Why did they want to know about me?" Another pause, and Kent said in a shaky voice, "No, no, don't worry. I won't call you—ever again." He hung up and walked out of the telephone office to the late bar opposite.

Shlomo saw that his sallow face had gone gray-white with fear and that his hand trembled almost uncontrollably as he wolfed down three Romagna brandies.

Steiger's going to love this, thought Shlomo. Is this guy guilty as hell!

Without pausing the man who called himself Kent and Bergman drank two thick double-strength coffees in quick succession, slumped in an aluminum chair at a little round table. He stared straight ahead and the shaking seemed to stop after a while. He had another brandy, and then the waiter came around busily sweeping under his feet—the Italian way of telling you the place is closing.

Kent wandered out into the street and down to the main via del Corso, almost deserted at two o'clock in the morning. He seemed to be walking aimlessly, with his head down, even forgetting his usual habit of glancing nervously over his shoulder from time to time. He turned up the via Borgognona, closed to traffic, where the store owners had laid a red carpet all the way up to the Piazza di Spagna and dotted benches and thick plant beds at intervals along the center of the street. On one of the benches was a courting couple who were going to have to reverse engines smartly if they didn't want to be arrested for public indecency. On another was a tramp snoring under a bundle of newspapers in the warm summer night.

Kent sat on one of the benches at the third clump of plants. He stayed completely still, his hands clasped in his lap, his chin resting on his chest—an old man in a crazy antique pinstripe suit with large pointed lapels.

The watchers in the gloom could not tell whether he was sleeping, or lost in some of the hardest thinking of his life.

Chapter Twenty-Two

By three in the morning at the Bellini Travel Office, Steiger already had the test-fired slugs from the .38. The tame forger had been given Kent's Residence Permit, had stuck his own picture on it and was working away at Kent's spidery signature.

There wasn't much anyone could do after that except watch Kent.

Steiger had been on his feet since six o'clock the previous morning, when word came from Tel Aviv that Kent was to be denounced, and so had Ran and many of the other people in the team.

Red-eyed, Steiger took a final knock-out shot of Scotch and decreed sleep in the armchairs around the office until Kent made another move—except for the duty man on the telephone.

But Ran seized the chance of following Zipporah into a side office.

"I didn't get a chance to thank you properly for fixing my leg," he said.

Zipporah stared back at him as if she were a professional nurse.

"How is it?"

"It will be fine. Look, Zipporah," said Ran, taking a step toward her and reaching out.

She shrank back and put out a hand as if to ward

him off. "I've told you I'm sorry about using you like that. It was just one of those things, and I'm getting over it now."

"I just wanted to tell you that I didn't mind being used at all—and that you can feel free to come over to my place any time—even if it's just to avoid being alone," said Ran. "I mean, I get lonely too in this business."

"I'm sorry," she said coldly, staring straight at him. "We all have to handle our problems as best we can. Thanks for the offer anyway—but I think we had all better concentrate on the job in hand." She walked out of the room, leaving Ran to wipe the egg off his face.

If that's what she's like when she's being friendly, what does she do to people she doesn't like? he asked himself as he collapsed into a chair and closed his eyes.

Back in the main office it seemed like twenty seconds before Steiger was awakened again, but he found he had managed seventy-five minutes sleep.

Shlomo was on the phone. "Kent's on the move again. He stayed on that bench for about two hours. He's walked up through the Piazza di Spagna onto the via Tritone, and now he's going up the via Barberini. It looks to me as if he could be heading for the main railway station. He's going along at quite a brisk clip."

While Kent had been dozing—or thinking—on the bench, Steiger had sent a relief man along to join Shlomo.

"The airline terminal is at the central railway station too, so he might be going for a train or a flight," said Steiger. "If he books on anything I'll want you to go with him and have the relief man call me. I had planned to leave him on and let you get away for some sleep, but I'm afraid you'll have to stick with it now."

"I'll manage," said Shlomo. "If this is who we think he is, I wouldn't be able to sleep anyway, worrying in case he gives us the slip."

Twenty minutes later Shlomo was back on. "He's bought a second class ticket, one-way to Chiasso. And the next train leaves at 5:40."

"Where the hell is Chiasso?" asked Steiger, grabbing a map.

"It's about thirty miles north of Milan—and it's the border crossing point into Switzerland," said Shlomo. "There's something else. He has to change trains in Milan—there's a half-hour break there. But the one up to Chiasso goes on to Lugano and Zurich."

Shlomo didn't yet know that Kent had a tidy sum in a Zurich bank.

"Where does the train stop?" asked Steiger.

Shlomo read him the timetable. There was a one-minute stop at Arezzo, probably to throw off and take on the mail that the Italian postal system seemed to pulp rather than deliver these days. Then there were regular ten-minute stops at Florence and Bologna before Milan. After that it only stopped at Como before the border checkpoint at Chiasso, where it was due at 2:18 in the afternoon.

"How much was his ticket?"

"Seven thousand, seven hundred lire—that's a bit over five pounds," said Shlomo.

Steiger thought it over. Kent must really be strapped for ready cash by now after his big bender with the girl and a couple of restaurant lunches. Maybe he had a few Swiss francs around to buy his onward ticket from Chiasso, if Zurich was where he was going. He had bought the cheapest possible ticket, so the chances were he intended to use it all the way.

"What's Kent doing now?" he asked.

"He's at the station coffee shop stepping outside a coffee and a roll."

"I'll have another man down there in ten minutes.

209

That'll make three of you. If he really gets on the train, have the third man call me immediately. That leaves two of you to keep after him. If he gets off at Arezzo, Florence or Bologna, call me and I'll organize reliefs. We are O.K. in Milan and can have two men to meet you there while he changes trains. I'll have them stand on the right side of the platform exit and they'll both be carrying—Zipporah, what's a Milan morning newspaper—yes, they'll both be carrying a copy of *Il Giorno* in their right hands and you two carrying *Messaggero* in your right hands. You'll see them easier than they see you, so you start the code approach. It will be —er, let's see—'How much is lunch at the station buffet?' and the answer is 'The hunting season's just opened.'

"One of the Milan men will get on with you and the other will call me when we know if he's really bolting for Switzerland. The main thing I want is for at least two of you to be with this joker at all times, from now on. I see there's a twenty-minute stop at Chiasso, so one of you can call me from there, too,"

Steiger checked that both men had passports and plenty of money.

Shlomo asked him what he should do about the .22 pistol in his pocket.

"Give it to the man I'm sending down now. No artillery for this job. Kent's unarmed now and we don't want any ugly scenes at the border if you're searched. We can arrange to get some shooters to you in Switzerland if necessary."

A few minutes later, Joe Burke got a phone call from one of the two British agents slogging around after the Israelis and Kent. "It's all happening," said the man. "Kent bought a ticket for somewhere or other but we couldn't see where. Can't get too close to him or the Israelis will notice us. But the Israelis have just bought themselves two second-class singles to Chiasso. I guess that's where Kent's going."

"Brilliant, Dr. Watson," said Burke. "What time's the train leaving?"

"In twenty minutes."

"Damn—no time to get an extra man down there. Right. I'll assume that if I haven't heard from you within half an hour you are both on the train with him. And I'll get Fred to meet you in Milan if Kent hasn't hopped off in between."

Ten minutes later Kent walked out of the station coffee shop and boarded the train for Chiasso. He wandered down the second-class coaches and took a forward facing corner seat. The only exits were at each end of the coach.

The train left on time.

In eight and a half hours it would be at the Swiss border.

Steiger sent an urgent cable to the Chief telling him that as far as he now knew, the Israelis were the only people who knew where Kent was and that the Italian police were hopelessly late in acting on the extradition request from Germany. Steiger no longer doubted that Kent was in fact Wagner, and he reckoned he could have the hundred percent proof the Prime Minister had demanded once he had a ballistics report and had peeked inside Kent's strong box in the Banco della Mercede. There would be a third check, via Tel Aviv, on whether such a man as Alfred Herbert Kent had been born in Wichita Falls in 1906. But that would come later, as it was now the middle of the night in Texas.

As the Israelis seemed to be managing quite nicely again, Steiger told the Chief that he had no intention of tipping the Italians off on where they could find Kent. If Kent did slip into Switzerland a whole new set of rules would apply—and the Institute might still be able to handle things their way.

The strong box raiding party, the forger and some minders, were told to be at the bank one hour after opening time.

Half an hour later Eli was sent off to find an Inspector in the Rome Flying Squad who was discreet and friendly to the Israelis.

Detective Inspector Giancarlo Bertone looked and acted like any other Roman cop. He had the heavy build and suspicious look of a forty-five year old who had spent a quarter of a century dealing with thieves and murderers. Too young to fight in the war, he had finished a scrappy secondary school education and then got taken on at the police school a couple of years after the shooting stopped. He had been brought up a good Catholic, mostly by his father's sister. His mother had died when he was eight. From that age until Mussolini and the Blackshirts were defeated his father and aunt had told him never to talk about his mother to anyone, not even his closest friends at school.

For Bertone's mother had been Jewish.

The way the Jews saw it, that made Bertone a Jew, because the only sure definition of a Jew is someone born of a Jewish mother. Being pragmatic, the Jews reckon you always know who someone's mother is. You can never be quite sure about the father.

At Hitler's insistence, Mussolini had given Italian Jews a hard time during the war. They were expropriated, arrested, and some were deported.

But Bertone's father had moved from Bologna to Rome during the war, and no one ever remembered about Bertone's mother. Except Bertone—who bitterly resented having to be secretive about the woman who had lavished undemanding affection on him for the first eight years of his life until she died in childbirth.

Even after the war he noticed there was a lot of unofficial anti-Semitism in the police force. A lot of cops had been sympathetic to, if not active as, Fascists during the Mussolini regime. And they were top men in the force now.

Bertone decided he would still not shout about his parentage. But he realized at an early age what it would mean to be in a place where it wouldn't matter.

It turned out in 1948 that Israel was that place. But a lot of people were determined Israel should disappear off the map.

Just after the Six Day War in 1967, Bertone took the plunge. He contacted an Israeli journalist he had met in Rome on news stories—whom he knew was just a little better informed than an ordinary newspaperman—and told him that if he could ever do anything for the Jews he was willing to help.

At that time there wasn't much he could do. But as the Arab terrorists moved into Europe and the Institute expanded its network there to combat them, Bertone had become a key man.

When Arab terrorists were arrested in Rome—and invariably released on bail because of Italian oil interests' pressure on the Governments of the day—Bertone could tell the Institute where the released Arabs had gone, and could supply fingerprints. The terrorists might reappear later with different identities in another European country, and sometimes the Institute's men were waiting for them with their .22 special pistols.

Eli found Bertone this morning gulping a cappuccino in his usual cafe before heading for the Questura. He saw Eli and headed out after him to another cafe a hundred yards away.

Over two more cappuccini, with the fluffy milk just

213

right so that the sugar stayed on top for several seconds before sinking, Eli said, "Giancarlo, how are they getting on with the ballistics tests on Katz?"

"Should be finished by tonight. Two of the bullets stayed inside him and didn't hit any bones, so they are in good shape. But I'm afraid we have no ideas and we are looking for no suspects. They all reckon it was an Arab job, so I'm afraid no one's looking too hard. You know how it is—they just don't want to get involved."

"I thought so," muttered Eli. "Bunch of goddam goof-offs. Look, I've got a little something here for you."

He held a test-fired slug from Kent's revolver in the palm of his hand so that only Bertone could see, dropped it in a cigarette packet and passed it over to him.

"My God, that's quick," said Bertone. "What is it—Arabs, you reckon?"

"Dunno," said Eli. "Maybe, but if you can phone the usual number with a yes or no on comparisons as soon as possible it will help us one helluva lot."

"Will do," said Bertone, and lumbered out with that gait peculiar to policemen everywhere.

In the Travel Office, Steiger slammed the phone down on the cradle and said, "Shit—goddam Italians. Don't they ever work?"

He glared round at Ran and Zipporah. "That was the strongbox team calling from outside the bank. They've got a wildcat one-day strike down there. We can't even try to get in till tomorrow morning."

Chapter Twenty-Three

Bertone called Eli back at midday.

"The damndest thing happened," he said. "The Flying Squad got a telex passed on to them by the Foreign Ministry from Bonn asking us to pick up some kind of bum here that the Germans reckoned is Heinz Wagner."

He paused to let the effect sink in.

Eli tried to sound surprised. "Well, how about that. What are you doing about it?"

"Well," said Bertone, "I got myself assigned to it and we zoomed down with three squad cars to this place near the Piazza Navona, but the bird has flown. No sign of him there, no one's seen him this morning, and he isn't on the Piazza Navona, where he apparently flogs balloons and kids' toys. We've got everything staked out, but something seems to have gone wrong. A bunch of Kraut experts from Berlin have just arrived at the Questura with pictures of the guy and a full dossier, and they can't figure out why we didn't move on the request sooner. Looks like a cock-up in getting the telex from the Foreign Ministry to the Questura. I gather there's a right old row going on with the Germans suspecting some Fascist here tipped the suspect off and our Foreign Ministry sarcastically suggesting it's just possible that some Nazi in Germany got word to him."

Eli pretended he was taking notes, as Bertone gave him all the details about Kent.

Bertone said there was no trace of Kent in the Foreign Section's files at Headquarters, after he was issued a Residence Permit. "He should have told us about his change of address, but you know how it is. There are so many foreigners living here, legally and illegally, we'd be doing nothing else if we kept going around checking on them all. He hasn't made any waves, so we've had no reason to go looking for him."

Bertone said that the man had been given his Residence Permit on the basis of an American passport, and a letter from the American Express saying he was employed as a tour guide.

"The American Express tell us they had a man of that name working with them from 1958 to 1961, but they don't know why he left."

"Maybe he'll show up back at home later today," ventured Eli.

"Maybe," said Bertone. "But I'll tell you something else. The Foreign Ministry are so afraid they'll get raw egg on their face on this one that they've churned up the Carabinieri and got the Defense and Interior Ministries warning customs and police at all border points to look for him.

"They're checking through this morning's flights at Fiumicino, but they only have the passenger lists to work on—people don't fill out exit forms when they leave Italy, so he could be on his way somewhere already. But they're so stirred up they're wiring pictures of this guy to all the border checkpoints too, right now."

"Hmm," said Eli. "Well, as you can imagine, we have more than a passing interest in this one. Let us know how you get on.

"By the way," he added casually, "how did you get on with the ballistics thing?"

"No time yet," said Bertone. "They've got me full-time on this Wagner thing—I'm at the Piazza Navona right now. But I'll get to the laboratory tonight or first thing in the morning."

It was only after he hung up that Bertone realized he had been asked to make a ballistics check on a bullet pulled out of an Israeli killed only yards from where a man believed to be Heinz Wagner lived. And he'd read the night report on a strange incident in the same area in which a youth had crashed on a motor scooter and was still in hospital in a coma.

Eyewitnesses had told a confused story about a pillion passenger on the motor scooter being bundled into a nearby car by a short, dark man waving a gun.

He looked at his watch.

It was twelve-fifteen, and the balloon man was huddled in his second class coach window seat staring out over the Lombardy plain, forty-five minutes from Milan and just over two hours from the Swiss frontier. Shlomo and the second Institute man were on the corridor side at each end of the same coach, and two English "businessmen" were in the compartment next door.

At the gigantic and gloomy Milan Central Station, Kent walked slowly down the platform. If he was going to contact anyone, this was his last chance before the border.

The Israelis and the British got their separate signals right and joined up with their agents sent down to the station. One of each group ran to the telephones to tell their offices that Kent had arrived.

Kent squinted up at the departures board and saw that train 380 was leaving on schedule from platform 8 for Zurich in twenty minutes.

Then he dived into the public washrooms, closely escorted by an Israeli and a Briton, apparently simultaneously afflicted by full bladders.

But Kent dropped no paper, picked nothing up and spoke to no one on his way to or from the lavatory stalls.

He got on the Zurich-bound express with five minutes to spare after buying himself a plastic-wrapped salami sandwich from a man wheeling a mobile buffet along the platform. No messages were exchanged between Kent and the salesman except the customary *"Grazie"* and *"Prego."* And Shlomo, watching hawk-eyed, saw that Kent dropped the exact amount of four hundred-lire pieces into the outstretched palm—no pieces of paper.

As the train pulled out of the station the Institute men were as sure as they could be that Kent had contacted no one since the phone call at two o'clock in the morning to his erstwhile call-girl friend.

Forty-three minutes later, the express stopped briefly at Como after glimpses of one of Italy's most fabulous lakes. A horde of border police, customs men and Carabinieri in their distinctive black-and-red-striped uniforms with the flaming torch cap badges boarded the train as it jerked its way slowly onto the border checkpoint at Chiasso three miles away. Lake Como disappeared on the right as the frontier guards tapped their way through the compartments checking passports and opening an occasional suitcase.

Chiasso is a typical border town with the frontier going slap through the middle. Its chief claim to fame is that it is the closest possible international border to Milan and Rome. The Swiss side is bulging with branches of all the main banks, waiting for wealthy Italians or their emissaries to stagger through with the millions of lire they are not prepared to declare to the taxman—or their wives—and which they instantly convert into Swiss francs at almost any rate of exchange.

Depending on the price of petrol and tobacco, it has also been a main crossing point for these commodities. And the Italian customs men are particularly hot on anyone coming in with salt.

The Government has a state monopoly on salt and tobacco, and visitors to Italy are perpetually puzzled when they are told they must buy salt at a tobacconist.

Usually Italian customs men are fairly relaxed with foreigners but give their own countrymen absolute hell.

After Como, Shlomo moved up the corridor to a point opposite Kent's compartment. The khaki-uniformed border guard on their coach had a Carabin-iere with him. That, thought Shlomo, was unusual, The para-military state police force didn't usually get in-volved in frontier checks.

Behind the two Italians the Swiss border guards were moving up too. Each side had a deal where the guards could board on each other's territory a few miles short of the border to save time.

Shlomo noticed Kent, still looking steadfastly out of the window, was licking his lips nervously as he heard the border men shouting "Passports, please" into each compartment. There were two other passengers sitting in Kent's compartment—each holding Italian pas-sports.

The train stopped with a jolt in Chiasso station. Sh-lomo saw that there were plenty more border guards and customs men walking up and down the platform. Steiger had told him from Rome that a special alert was out for Kent.

What no one knew up to that point was whether Kent had a passport, and if so, what name was in it.

"Passaporti," said the frontier policeman, peering into Kent's compartment. He turned over the two Ital-ian passports cursorily and looked at Kent.

The balloon man reached into his breast pocket and pulled out an olive green booklet with gold lettering on it—a United States passport.

The frontier guard flipped open the cover and looked at the name.

Behind him the Carabiniere constable was staring at Kent.

"Anything to declare?" said the frontier guard.

"No, nothing," said Kent.

"Where is your baggage, please?"

Kent said, "No baggage. I'm only going to Lugano for the day."

"Thank you," said the guard, handing back Kent's passport.

Shlomo strolled back up the corridor ahead of the guards as if to go into his own compartment. It looked as if Kent had made it.

But as he looked back, he saw the Carabiniere lean out of the coach window and signal to a sergeant. The sergeant and two more constables clambered aboard and moved down the coach.

There was a muttered conference and the sergeant studied a large photograph in his hand. He walked up and looked into Kent's compartment again.

With the constables tucked in behind him, he opened the door and walked in. Shlomo heard him say, "Passport, please," again.

The train was scheduled to stop for twenty minutes at Chiasso.

Shlomo decided it was time to get off. As he stood on the platform at one end of the coach, the other Israeli dropped off at the far exit and casually lit a cigarette.

Two minutes later, the sergeant got off. Then came Kent, and the three constables brought up the rear. They walked the thirty yards to the Carabinieri office on the station and disappeared inside. Shlomo walked down and said to the other man, "Stay and make sure they don't let him get back on."

Shlomo sidled past the Carabinieri Office, but the windows were frosted and he could not see inside.

He went to the long-distance phone in the station waiting room and called Steiger.

"They got him," he said. "I always did say there were only three things that worked in Italy—the motorway system, the Communist party, and the Carabinieri."

The train pulled out on time without Kent and without the two English businessmen who bustled off at the last second.

Thirty minutes later, Kent came out of the Carabinieri office flanked this time by two plainclothesmen. They walked to a chauffeured, unmarked Alfa Romeo outside the station entrance and, with a uniformed carabinieri escort in another Alfa, roared off down the road in the direction of the A.9 motorway for Milan and the southern motorway network.

On his next call, Steiger was able to tell Shlomo something. "Don't worry about losing him," he said. "Our Questura man tells us he's being flown back to Rome from Linate airport near Milan on the four o'clock plane. I don't reckon you two can make it, but we'll pick him up at Fiumicino. Come on the next plane after that, they run every hour or so."

"What happens now?" asked Shlomo.

"Dunno" grunted Steiger. "Bit disappointing, really. I thought we might have had Colonel Wagner all to our little selves again."

Chapter Twenty-Four

The Questura, Rome's Police Headquarters, is a gloomy building, like most police buildings around the world. An old block-long Palazzo, it has a large inner courtyard with steps and corridors going off in every direction.

Kent's detention had been sought by the Germans "with maximum discretion," but the Italian police were feeling pretty pleased that they had saved the Foreign Ministry from having to make some awkward explanations to the Germans. By the time Kent was driven into headquarters, the sharper boys in the permanent press office there had got the word that something pretty big was going on.

When Kent was hustled out of the car in the main yard, a photographer managed to loose off a fuzzy long-focus shot of the VIP prisoner and was hawking it around the Rome newspaper offices later that night. The reporters were going into ecstasies of speculation about who the prisoner might be, and the speculation ranged from a wanted top banker whose five banks had collapsed to the big man behind the kidnapping of Paul Getty III. But no one guessed it was a top Nazi war criminal—and the police wanted to be sure before making any really dramatic leaks.

They worked Kent over in shifts for three hours inside the Questura, with Inspector Bertone taking part in the relay questioning and calling Eli during the breaks.

"He's giving us a hard time," he told Eli. "He just sits there and keeps repeating the name on his passport as Alfred Herbert Kent. He says he was on his way to Switzerland for a little break and has a bit of money up there. He claims he has been in Italy since about five years after the war and had that job with the American Express, which as far as we can tell is true. He said he started hitting the bottle rather heavily and forgot to turn up for work a couple of times and the American Express finally told him not to bother to turn up at all. After that, he claims he bummed around Italy doing odd jobs and then started selling these balloons about six years ago. The people at the Piazza Navona certainly remember him being there that long, and the man who supplies his balloons and the hydrogen cylinder knows him. But he won't tell us who any of his friends are—says he hasn't got any. We're still having a go, and I'll let you know if there's a break. But he's certainly a tough old guy and doesn't give away more than he's asked—if that much. At the moment, the only technicality we have him on is failing to notify us of his change of address and loss of job. But for that, the most we can do is expel him."

Bertone said Kent spoke Italian with what could be a German accent, but there was no one around who spoke English or German fluently enough to be able to test him. They were planning to bring some of the people from the Berlin Prosecutor's Office in on the questioning to test him.

Eli asked him about the ballistics test.

"That's funny," said Bertone, "I could have sworn you were going to ask me about that. Your little sample is over with my friend in the police laboratory now.

By the way, you can do me a favor, too. Any ideas who would want to knock a couple of young cut-purses off their scooter near the Piazza Navona last night, half killing one of them and kidnapping the other?"

"Funny man," said Eli, and hung up.

He had just finished briefing Steiger and Ran on the interrogation so far when an urgent message arrived from Tel Aviv.

"Report from Wichita Falls says there are no city birth records from 1890 to 1910—period in which suspect says he was born. No record of birth in newspaper files. School officials say they have no record of a student by that name. Tax and other City records show no one of that name. Police Chief says he cannot locate anyone who remembers any man by that name."

Steiger whistled as he read the cable. "Looks like Alfred Herbert Kent is a figment of our friend's imagination, and I'm not giving any prizes in this office for guessing who he really is."

Steiger, Ran and even Zipporah laughed and poured themselves drinks to celebrate what looked like a coming break.

The next telephone call from Bertone brought them all down off the chandelier.

"That slug you passed me," he said. "There's no way it could have come out of the same gun that killed Katz. The rifling's totally different. My ballistics friend is absolutely certain. Sorry about that."

The intricate web Steiger and his men had been weaving seemed to be crumbling all of a sudden. Leaving Eli to wait for new calls from Bertone, there was nothing Steiger, Ran and Zipporah could do at that monent but go out in search of their first organized meal in two days. In a nearby trattoria a steaming bowl of *penne alla carbonara*, a kind of short macaroni with diced bacon and egg yolk sauce, washed down with a bottle of Chianti restored their flagging spirits a notch.

"Look at it this way," said Ran, "if Kent himself didn't kill Yossi, maybe a Nazi friend of his did."

Steiger pushed his *penne* around disconsolately. "I thought of that," he said. "But if he has such obliging friends who are prepared to switch off one of our guys just because they seem to be taking an interest in him, where were they when he really needed them to get out of the country. I'm damn sure he contacted no one here. He was going it entirely alone."

Zipporah had been listening quietly. She asked, "If Kent didn't kill Yossi, who did?"

"I think we'll have to get Tel Aviv to start checking on that claim by the Democratic Liberation Front that they killed Yossi in retaliation for the blowing up of Wasfi Aziz in Beirut. I personally don't believe they could have reacted that quickly, and I can only suppose they had been watching Yossi for some time anyway. The proximity of the two killings was a sheer coincidence, one that made us jump to the conclusion that Kent was the guilty party," said Steiger.

Ran stole a glance at Zipporah, who was looking down steadfastly into her plate again and not even offering further comment. She did not know that Ran had sent the fatal car to Wasfi Aziz in Beirut—but if she ever found out, she might in her heart blame Ran for triggering the retaliation against her man.

"Anyway," continued Steiger, pretending not to notice the sudden silence, "what are we left with? A mystery about Yossi, but that doesn't alter the fact that Kent is still a dead ringer for Wagner, he's been identified by Wagner's wife, he lived in fear and carried a gun, and he's so terrified of drawing attention to himself that he preferred to make a bolt for it rather than report he had been robbed."

By the end of the meal the three of them were still

convinced that the man arrested that afternoon was Colonel Heinz Wagner.

The feeling was boosted when they got back to the office and Eli told them that Bertone had called again to say German experts from Berlin and Italian police had ordered Kent to strip—and they had found an appendectomy scar.

Wagner had had an appendectomy in 1938.

Bertone reported later that the Italian police had now received a similar report to Steiger's. There was no record of an Alfred Herbert Kent ever having been born or lived in Wichita Falls. That made the Questura pretty confident they were on the right track and finally one interrogator came right out with it and said to Kent, "You are Heinz Wagner, aren't you?"

Kent had looked back and said, "I am who?"

"Heinz Wagner, SS Colonel Heinz Wagner—wanted for a small matter of killing ten million people in the last war," snapped the interrogator.

Bertone reported that Kent had looked down, his head casting a big shadow under the plain naked bulb of the interrogation room, sitting on an upright wooden chair as the interrogators stood round him, and started shaking uncontrollably.

Suddenly the other men in the room realized that Kent was laughing—but not in the ordinary way. He was laughing silently and then taking in great gobs of air before he started shaking again.

"Come on, get it off your chest. We know all about you," said one man, shaking Kent by his shoulders. But they couldn't stop the sallow, aging man from shaking.

"He went on for about five minutes," said Bertone. "And we finally got really alarmed. He was obviously in hysterics and we had to get the police doctor in to give him a shot. The doc said we'd have to let him sleep for a while, otherwise we might kill him. We've got him bedded down in a cot for the night and we are going to have another go first thing in the morning."

Steiger and his crew decided there was nothing more for them to do that night but get some sleep, too. As they were leaving the office Eli came in from a late night supper at about half past midnight and thrust a copy of the Rome morning paper *Messaggero* under their noses.

"Well, what do you think of that for Italian police discretion?" he groaned.

Splashed all the way over the front page was the banner headline "Heinz Wagner arrested?" And underneath were two gigantic pictures side by side. One was a newspaper file picture of Colonel Wagner. Beside it was the picture that had been radioed to frontier stations all over Italy earlier in the day. And although there were no direct quotes from the police, the *Messaggero* crime reporter had more or less got the whole story—adding his own flourishes and ornaments. It went all the way down page one and over to page five, with more wartime pictures of Wagner. The *Messaggero* people had worked fast. They knew about the German extradition request and even had the bit about Kent and Wagner both having appendectomies, which the police themselves had not known until two and a half hours before the paper hit the street.

"Oops," said Steiger. "The shit's really going to hit the fan now."

It certainly did.

During the night the Associated Press and United Press International picture services picked up the Kent photograph and wired it all over the world. Reuter got a quote out of a police spokesman down at the Questura saying that the *Messaggero* story was "substantially correct."

As the presumed Wagner was posing as an American, the story got top treatment in the United States as well as in Europe. By early morning, people picking up their morning papers were literally bludgeoned with the story and pictures.

Special correspondents from Germany, the United States, Israel, and anyone else who could afford the airfare were homing in on the Questura in Rome to be in at the death.

Next morning the Israeli Embassy spokesman, who never said much about anything anyway, came out with a guarded statement that "naturally Israel followed with close interest any developments which would tend to ensure the arrest of a man responsible for the death of ten million people, six million of them being Jews. In view of the German extradition request, Israel is not at the moment contemplating any extradition request of her own to try this man under our Genocide Law—if it emerges that he is indeed Heinz Wagner."

At the Bellini Travel Service the petty frustrations of Italy were still interfering with the Institute's parallel investigation. The banks were on strike for a second day and there was no way of looking into Kent's safe deposit box until the following morning, if the banks condescended to do business.

Now that word had got out, newspapermen were beginning to uncover additional details. Squads of them scoured Wichita Falls and no one could come up with any trace of Kent ever having been there.

Steiger himself decided to go down and hang around outside the Questura with the press. There were all three American TV networks there, Italian RAI TV, the BBC, ITN and the German networks.

Although Bertone told Eli that Kent himself had not requested it, the American Embassy in Rome sent down a consular official and police allowed him to speak to Kent.

After a ten-minute meeting, the lanky, bespectacled vice consul was swamped as he emerged from the Questura. Steiger, waving a pencil and notebook, eased forward in the crush as cameramen cursed and sound men unraveled their tangled wires.

The vice consul could not even reach his car and finally stopped. "Gentlemen," he said into the bank of cameras whirring like well-oiled coffee grinders, "I can only say that I asked this United States citizen if he required any assistance and that he is demanding his immediate release. Files at our Embassy show that he has at regular intervals been issued with a U.S. passport, and there is nothing to show that the original passport was irregularly obtained. Naturally we are checking that out with the State Department, where central records are held. That is all I can tell you."

As he started pushing towards his waiting car again, a CBS reporter jabbed a microphone under his nose and said, "Is he really American? How's his English?"

The vice consul stopped at the car door and turned. "In my opinion, he speaks with a perfect North American accent. I would add that he also seems to have a pretty good Texas drawl."

As he dived into the car another American reporter cracked, "How the hell would he know—he's from Boston," and there was a burst of guffaws.

Steiger was down in the dumps again as he headed for the office. He was wondering how a Nazi war criminal could cultivate an American accent with such a local flavor that he could fool an American consular officer.

By mid-morning there was more stunning news from Bertone.

"That vice consul told us he reckoned the man was a genuine American and warned that unless we could produce evidence to the contrary pretty quickly there might be some stiff notes flying back and forth. The Foreign Ministry is around our necks all the time. Kent seems to feel better after a night's sleep and is coming up with another story."

Kent had told the police that what he had done in the past was his business, provided he had broken no Italian laws. But just to help them, he said they could check with the United Fruit Company, who used to practically run Guatemala. He said that he was employed by United Fruit for about six months in the last half of 1942. "He even said he left three days before Christmas in that year," says Bertone. "And he claims that the Company records will show that."

Urgent cables had gone off through Interpol to Guatemala City and United Fruit's records office, and now everyone was leaving Kent alone while they waited for the reply—probably the next day.

Gloom descended in the Bellini Travel Office.

Steiger said, "I doubt whether he'd claim he'd been in Central America during the war unless he really was and expects to be able to prove it."

Ran riffled through the Wagner file. There were dates and pictures of him in the last half of 1942 in his SS Colonel's uniform in Russia, Poland, Berlin, Czechoslovakia, and inspecting several concentration camps.

In London, unaware that the whole case against Kent seemed to be rapidly falling apart, Miriam Goldhill called her husband in the office.

"Sam," she said excitedly, "get hold of the *Evening Standard*. They've got the story about that man I thought was Wagner all over the front page. He's been arrested and there are pictures and everything."

"Good God," said Sam, "has he confessed?"

"No, no—but I'm absolutely sure it's him. You've only got to look at the pictures they've dug up. Wait till I tell our friends about this."

A warning bell sounded in Sam's head.

"I wouldn't do that if I were you, dear. There are still a lot of people around who do not like people who denounce Nazi war criminals."

"Oh, come on, Sam, this is marvelous. It's a lifetime's dream come true to nail that swine. I'm going to invite the Halsmanns and the Winegreens over to dinner this very night to tell them the whole story. And I promise not to tell them the part about you trying to talk me out of it," she laughed, as she hung up.

Chapter Twenty-Five

The streets of Rome were melting the next morning under the stultifying July sun. The Romans were even slower-moving than usual as Steiger negotiated his giant frame to the Travel Office.

The only good news of the morning was that the banks were open and the forger was going to try for the bank vault and Kent's box. He left with Ran as back-up man and Eli as driver of the getaway car, in case something went wrong.

"For God's sake don't get this one wrong," warned Steiger. "We are managing to keep our outfit out of this fairly well so far, and if there's the slightest suspicion of the forger, or the teller goes off to make a check, just get out of there as fast as you can. And nobody—but nobody—is to get hurt. No guns to be used and no karate chops, just a fast withdrawal as best you can."

Steiger had seriously thought of postponing the bank job. But as he said to Ran, "Everyone is doing a great job of negative vetting on this man. They are just gathering evidence that he may not be Wagner. But the only way to be sure he isn't Wagner is to find out who he really is—and one guy I'm sure he's not is Alfred Herbert Kent. It looks as if we are going to have to do our own positive vetting."

Half an hour later, Ran and the forger got out of Eli's car at the Banco della Mercede. There was a small, crowded parking lot on one side, and Eli backed in so that he was facing out onto the via del Corso.

The forger went in first with a camera-packed brief-case and Ran followed two seconds later. He hung back unconcernedly picking his teeth as the forger walked over to the entrance to the vault section, but the pick snapped under the tension. The forger handed Kent's identity card with his superimposed picture on it to the vault teller, and the Bank Certificate showing he held a safe deposit box there.

The Kent-Wagner story had been all over the Italian papers. It all now depended on whether the teller read newspapers closely—or at all—and on whether Kent had been a frequent visitor to the vaults and was remembered.

The teller looked at the two identity documents and looked up at the forger. He passed across a slip for the forger to sign to gain admission to the vaults. Then he compared the signatures. He smiled at the forger and said, "Got your key?"

Obviously not an ardent newspaper reader.

As the forger waved his key, the teller swung open the heavy vault door and handed him over to the man inside the vault with the master key. Ran breathed a sigh of relief as he disappeared, and almost got himself ulcers thinking of the wait until the man came out.

Inside the vaults, the master-key operator walked along two rows and stopped at vault number 84682. The operator and the forger both inserted their keys and turned. In ten more seconds, the Israeli agent had the long narrow metal box in his hand and had been ushered into a private inspection compartment.

He lifted the box lid.

It was almost empty—no wads of banknotes, no gold

bars, no gems.

Lying in the bottom was an envelope containing several sheets of white paper with handwriting on one side.

That was all.

The forger laid the envelope and sheets out on the table, carefully adjusted the curtain behind him and pulled a camera and a bright battery-operated lamp out of his briefcase. Flashbulbs might have attracted the vault guard's curiosity.

It took five minutes' work with a close-up lens to photograph all the sheets three times each, reseal the envelope and return it to the box.

In another three minutes he was back out in the street, climbing into Eli's car with Ran. The forger only spoke Italian, and Eli said, "So what's in there?"

"Just some bits of paper, no money or anything like that. I don't know what was written on the paper—it was all in English."

The three men rocketed back to the office and the forger went down to the laboratory in the cellar to work on the photographs.

Ran bounded into Steiger's room. "We made it," he said. "Got clean away. No money or anything like that, but something in English handwriting. I'll belt back down to the cellar to grab the pictures when they are ready."

"Nice work, Ran," grinned Steiger as Ran hurried out.

The smile faded abruptly as Eli came in and said, "I just got a call from Bertone as I walked in the door. The bad news is that both Guatemala and United Fruit confirm that an Alfred Herbert Kent, born 1909 in Wichita Falls, was employed from May to December of 1942. The further bad news is that the Guatemalans even found on file a right index fingerprint taken for his local I.D. card at the time, and radioed it to the Questura. It matches the right index finger print they took off Kent this morning. There's no good news."

Steiger and Zipporah just stared at Eli, who shrugged his shoulders soundlessly.

After that things went pretty fast.

The Questura made a public announcement that they were satisfied that Kent was not Wagner, that they were releasing him that afternoon and that he would be escorted to the border because he was in the country illegally, having failed to fulfill residence requirements —a face-saver for the police.

The police and Foreign Ministry quickly shifted the blame onto the Germans, saying they had only been doing their best to help a neighbor and ally. The Berlin Public Prosecutor's Office said their tip-off "came from a reliable source and fully justified our action in securing the detention of a man who might have been a major Nazi war criminal." And they leaked the information that the tip had come from Paul Baurdoux in Paris.

Baurdoux's Institute contact just managed to restrain the enraged ex-deportee from blowing the whistle on the Israelis.

By midday, just about everybody involved had egg on their faces.

Steiger had just finished drafting his message to the Chief in Tel Aviv with the disastrous news, when Ran walked in the door holding the prints of the documents found in Kent's strongbox.

He looked at Steiger with a quizzical glance as he tosssd the sheets onto his desk.

"Just who the hell," he asked, "was Sir Harry Oakes?"

Chapter Twenty-Six

Steiger looked down at the photocopies. There was writing on the picture of the envelope which said, "To be opened in the event of my death." The writing was spidery and similar to the signature by Kent on his electricity contract form.

The writing on the sheets of paper was headed: "To the F.B.I., Washington, D.C., U.S.A." It was undated.

"I, the undersigned, John Charles Quaranta, swear by God that I am the man who killed Sir Harry Oakes at Nassau in the Bahamas on the night of July 7th, 1943. The one who ordered me to do it was Enzo Trombetta—they call him Eddie the Trumpet in the papers. I don't know for sure why I was told to do it, but I read in the papers afterwards where Trombetta was trying to get the tables into Nassau and this Oakes was trying to stop him. Trombetta paid me ten thousand dollars before the job and he was going to give me ten grand afterwards but I never got the other half. This is why. Three of us ran a cabin cruiser into Nassau from Miami on the afternoon of July 7th. We got in O.K. and the Bahamas police didn't see us. I went ashore and the other two guys had to wait for me. Trombetta told me it had to look like an accident so I couldn't use a gun. Oakes lived at a house called Westbourne near the Bahamas Country Club. I had to wait around outside as he had friends for dinner but they all left by eleven. Then I saw lights going on and off. But I knew Oakes was in the bedroom in the southwest corner. I saw his lights go out about eleven-thirty, but then there was someone in a bedroom along the balcony on the southeast corner. I later saw it was some friend of his, Harold Christie. In a few minutes this Christie's lights went out too and I waited maybe an hour. The front door was open so I went up the steps and into Oakes' bedroom. He was asleep and I brought a big poker from the boat. I only hit him once on the head through the mosquito net and he didn't move. I started to fix it to look like a fire. I found a broom in the cupboard and set a match to it. I dabbed the lighted broom around the bed and set light to the mosquito netting and then the broom fell on Oakes in the bed. He was still alive and rolled off on the floor groaning. He was bleeding from the head and I grabbed the poker again and hit him two or three more times. After that he didn't move any more and I heaved him back onto the bed. But I got blood on my pants and hands. While I was trying to light up the room again poking the broom at the mattress, carpet and a screen in the corner I heard this other man moving around at the other end of the house. I figured it was time to leave so I went back down the stairs waving the broom around and firing anything I could see. When I got back to the boat around five in the morning I told these other two—Giuseppe Zampelli and Dante Pontecorvo—that it was all O.K. and the house was on fire. It took a day back to Miami and when I got there I found it all went wrong, the house didn't burn and they knew it was murder. I got sent for by Trombetta, who doesn't like bad mistakes. I knew he wasn't going to give me the other half of the money for the job and I knew what he did to someone else who got it wrong so I took off. Trombetta's been looking for me ever since. They nearly caught up with me a couple of times but I still had this passport in the name of Kent I used to get a job down in Guatemala before I went on the Trombetta payroll. Since the job I worked in Chicago, L.A. and Dallas. I stayed clean but I kept thinking it was them after me—so I came to Italy, where my folks came from. I speak Italian good and got a job at the American Express. But one of the people there started taking too much interest in where I was from, so I had to leave. I saved the money from the job and other things and I get them to send it to me every month. I was sick a couple of times, too. I know they are going to get me in the end but if they do, so help me God, I want you to know it was Trombetta that did it."

The rambling, ill-phrased letter was signed, "John C. Quaranta."

Steiger finished reading and looked up at Ran, Eli, Shlomo, Zipporah and the forger, who had all come into the office.

He let out a big sigh. "I'm afraid we've had it wrong all along," he groaned. "This man is a Mafia punk who made a bad mistake nearly thirty years ago—and he's been on the run ever since. This is a confession to one of the great unsolved murder mysteries—I remember it well—and that's why he's been walking around terrified and carrying a gun. The only similarity between him and Wagner is they are both murderers and they resemble each other. It's just that Wagner killed about ten million more people than this man."

It took about two hours to run down some files on the Oakes murder, which had occupied thousands of columns of newsprint at the time. Briefly, American-born Sir Harry Oakes, a mining magnate reputed to be the wealthiest man in Canada after prospecting there, had settled in the Bahamas just before the war and bought up a third of New Providence Island on which Nassau, the capital of the then British Island Colony, stood. His great friends were Harold Christie, the Bahamian Real Estate dealer through whom he bought his land—and the Duke of Windsor, appointed Governor of the Islands during the war, reputedly because Churchill wanted him to be kept out of the way of possible German overtures or a kidnap attempt.

Christie often used to spend the night at Oakes's luxurious home. On July 7th, 1943, some dinner guests had been invited to Westbourne. They all left by eleven. The servants had already left at ten. Later Christie was to say he bade Oakes goodnight as Oakes was climbing into bed and then went to his own room, where he read for a few minutes before falling asleep.

He said he woke twice during the night, once because he was bothered by mosquitoes and switched on the light to chase them from under his net, and once because of a thunderstorm.

At seven-thirty the next morning, he found the bludgeoned and charred body of Oakes on his bed.

For still unexplained reasons the Duke of Windsor as Governor called in Miami police to investigate what he described as a "suicide." Captain James Otto Barker and Captain Edward Walter Melchen flew over. After a day's investigations, Barker claimed a fingerprint he had found on the Chinese screen in Oakes's bedroom corresponded to one of the fingers of Oakes's son-in-law Mauritius Count Alfred de Marigny, whose marriage to his eighteen-year-old daughter Nancy he had violently opposed.

De Marigny was arrested and later tried for the murder. But his able defense counsel tore the shoddy and suspect police work by the Miami investigators to shreds in the Nassau courtroom, and the jury acquitted de Marigny on November 11th by a nine to three majority.

Attempts to reopen the investigation failed throughout the years. Police Captain Barker was shot dead nine years later by a bullet fired by his son in what was described as "justifiable homicide." An American woman lawyer, Betty Renner, who had worked for the FBI and who came to probe the murder seven years after it happened, was found stripped and murdered. And so was Harold Christie's personal secretary.

Captain Melchen, the Duke of Windsor and Harold Christie are now all dead of natural causes. Melchen said the Duke had called him in Miami to come and investigate a "suicide." The Duke never in his lifetime explained why he thought a bludgeoned and charred corpse could be a suicide.

One thing was sure—too many questions or too close an involvement in the Oakes murder had habitually led to violent death.

And now here was another terrified man, writing in his own way that the Mafia were trying to get gambling permits in Nassau during the war.

An American ex-FBI man and trial lawyer, Marshall Houts, had even claimed in his book *King's X* that the big Mafia money man Meyer Lansky had sent some men to persuade Oakes to use his influence to get Lansky a gambling license. But according to this version, there had been a violent row—and Oakes was struck and killed by mistake. Houts claimed that informants had said Oakes's body had been deliberately mutilated to strike terror in the hearts of anyone else who stood in the way of a gambling license. But that contradicted Houts' own earlier claim that Oakes had been murdered accidentally.

The scribbled confession by Quaranta-cum-Kent— that it was a bungled attempt to look like an accident and that another big Mafioso had decided Oakes should die anyway—made a lot more sense.

But for the disappointed men in the room at the Bellini Travel Service, it all added up to one thing. They had been wasting months of their time on a man they thought was Wagner—and might have lost one of their best men because of his failure to watch his back properly against ambushing Arabs.

The phone rang. It was Bertone.

"We are going to release Kent in twenty minutes," he said. "He has no money left and has asked to be taken to the Swiss border, where he has an account. So we are sending him up there by train under escort. He will be expelled at Domodossola—but no one else knows that," he confided.

"You know something," Steiger said to Ran, "I've wasted all this time on this man, but I've never actually clapped eyes on him. I think I'm going down to see."

They climbed into the car and Eli drove them to the Questura.

They were just in time. The balloon man's few belongings had been collected from his attic near the Piazza Navona, and a plainclothesman walked out carrying his suitcase to a waiting police car. Reporters and cameramen surged forward. Everyone was screaming at once as Kent, his pinstripe suit making him sweat, blinked in the bright daylight.

"How does it feel to beat a charge of being Wagner?" "Who are you really?" "What are your plans now?" they screamed.

The man they all thought was called Kent brushed them aside as he climbed into the squad car. "I'm nobody, I got no background, I didn't do nothin'," he drawled. "You can say I'm a bum if you like. Now just leave me alone."

He sank back in the seat and closed his eyes. With police officers running interference to stop scooter-

241

mounted photographers from following, the squad car vanished around the corner.

Steiger walked disconsolately back to the office and called in Ran.

"Well," he said, "I'll have to file the final report now telling the Chief we've all been wasting our time chasing after a Mafia button man who balled up a murder thirty years ago."

"It's strange," said Ran. "Here we've solved what was one of the greatest murder mysteries of all time involving the former King of England—and we're saying we wasted our time. Someone must be interested in this guy. What about the British? Or this Mafioso Trombetta? Should we get the word to them?"

"To hell with the Brits," growled Steiger. "I don't feel like handing them the results of two months' hard work on a plate. And anyway, the Bahamas are independent now. I don't think the British could act on it anymore. And we are certainly not going to start helping Mafia chieftains track down a man they've been trying to bump off for thirty years. No, my friend, I'm afraid this is one for our files. Some day we may trade the information off with the British and they might be able to do themselves some good with the Bahamian authorities. And maybe the Bahamians don't want to drag the Oakes murder up again."

Over at the British Embassy Keane and Burke got the report from their Questura contact that the man they knew as Kent had been taken to the border for expulsion.

"That's bad luck for him," said Keane. "An old guy minding his own business getting chucked out just because the Israelis thought he was a big war criminal. They must still be wondering just who killed their man near the Piazza Navona, though. Do you think we should put them out of their misery and tell 'em?"

"To hell with the Israelis," said Burke. "We're not going to hand them anything on a plate. When we need something from them, I'll think about trading the information we have on who killed Katz."

Burke looked at his watch. "Just got time to tell London we've all been wasting our time, whoever this lad was—and then you can buy me lunch."

Chapter Twenty-Seven

At the railway station of Iselle, high up in the Italian Alps, the train came to a halt with squealing brakes early in the morning. It was the last halt before the train plunged into the Simplon Tunnel—at twelve miles and 560 yards, the world's longest—on its way into Switzerland. Although the air was crisp at two thousand feet at that hour, there was no snow in the summer, and the Simplon Pass with its pine-covered slopes was at its most majestic.

But a lot of drivers feared the hairpin bends and others were just lazy. At Iselle a series of flatcars are hooked on to the passenger coaches to be trundled through to Brig on the Swiss side of the pass. Fearful or hurried drivers can be towed through the dark tunnel for five or six pounds.

When the balloon man and his police escort arrived at Iselle the detective leaned out into the coach corridor where Italian and Swiss border police and customs men were checking the passenger compartments. To the Italian border guard he said, "Got an expellee here. This is his passport. And here's the expulsion order."

The guard signed the order. "What'd he do?"

"Well," said the escort, "they thought he'd done a lot of things but it all turned out wrong—so far as we're concerned, he just forgot to renew his residence permit, so out he must go."

The guard looked up the corridor to where the Swiss border policeman was working his way through the passengers. "Do I tell him about it?"

The detective looked at his watch. "Do me a favor," he said. "I don't have to be back in Rome till tomorrow night on this job, and I have hotel expenses. There's a bird I know in Milan. If the Swiss make trouble and delay him here while they check with Berne, I'll have to stay with him too—see what I mean?"

The border guard laughed and looked in at the man the Italians knew as Kent. He was sitting quietly in the corner seat with his head back against the rest after the journey through the night, his battered suitcase in the rack above him.

"O.K.," said the guard. "I won't spoil your date— and what the Swiss don't know won't hurt them."

He leaned into the compartment and handed Kent's passport to him.

"You must stay on this train, Signor Kent, until at least the next station in Switzerland. That's Brig. Do not attempt to get off here. We shall be keeping an eye on you."

Kent took his passport just in time to be able to offer it to the Swiss guard who had reached the compartment. The Swiss leafed through it briefly and handed it back without a word as the Italian detective walked back down the corridor with the Italian guard and got off the train. He and his "prisoner" had been in the last coach and now the flat cars which were to take the automobiles through the Simplon were being coupled on.

The detective and the guard stood on the platform waiting for the train to leave and making sure no one got off. The car drivers who had already been through customs and passport checks drove cautiously onto the flat cars, clattering over the heavy metal flanges which turned the flat cars into one long caterpillar. The first aboard was a large black Fiat hearse complete with an enormous and elaborately carved oak coffin in the back.

A train guard beckoned the hearse up to the front of the caterpillar and shouted to the two black-clad undertakers in the front seat. "Brakes on, car in gear, don't start the engine in the tunnel, and no lights on."

The driver nodded and lit a cigarette.

Behind the hearse came a large black Cadillac with two more men in dark suits and black ties followed by a string of cars with foreign number-plates.

The detective nodded at the hearse. "Are they taking someone or going to fetch them?"

"The stiff's right in the box now," said the guard. "A rich old Swiss banker's wife of eighty who snuffed it in a Milan hotel. Her old man wants her back in the family plot in Geneva. But the undertakers are a bunch of Sicilians, so I can tell you the customs boys made 'em unscrew the lid just to be sure she's in there and not a box full of cocaine."

The detective laughed, and the hearse driver glared at him.

A whistle blew and the train started off with a jerk. The detective and the frontier guard watched it disappear into the black hole of the Simplon before turning away.

In his compartment, the man they had thought was Wagner, and whom only the Israelis knew had in fact murdered Sir Harry Oakes, breathed an audible sigh of relief. The bespectacled maiden lady sitting opposite looked up from her detective novel for a second and then looked down again, straining to read the words in the gloomy compartment light. A man wearing a beret snored in the opposite corner.

About half a mile into the tunnel the compartment door opened.

A big man in a dark suit and fedora walked in and sat down next to Kent. Another equally large man hovered in the doorway.

The fedora hat leaned over and said quietly, "Mr. Kent?"

The balloon man looked at him, startled. "What do you want?"

The fedora hat flourished a wallet under his nose and said, "Swiss police. Come with us, please."

"Oh, Christ—I thought everyone would leave me alone. Now what, for God's sake?"

"Just a few formalities. Bring your suitcase too, please."

The balloon man stood up wearily as the big man pulled his case down from the rack.

The beady-eyed maiden lady watched the three men leave the compartment and turn towards the back of the train.

She had caught the words "Swiss police" and permitted herself a small shiver as she wondered who the man opposite her had been.

The other passenger snored on.

At that very moment Miriam Goldhill looked up from the newspaper she was reading at breakfast opposite her husband Sam. What she had read did not please her. The man she had first reported to the Israelis as being Colonel Heinz Wagner had turned out to be just an out-of-work American hobo. And the night before she had spent hours telling the Winegreens and the Halsmanns how she had first spotted the suspect.

This morning Sam had not mentioned the subject to her—although even in the *Financial Times* news sum-mary on page one there was a brief item headed, "Wagner suspect in Rome cleared."

Miriam clattered about with a coffee cup and finally said, "Well, all right. So we made a mistake."

Sam noticed it was now "we" who had got it wrong.

"Yes, dear, it looks as if we did," he said mildly.

"But anyway," blurted Miriam defensively, "he's only being thrown out of Italy—and he didn't have much of a job there. He can sell balloons anywhere—so I don't reckon we did him much harm."

"No, dear," said Sam, sorry for his wife's loss of face in front of their friends, but secretly hoping this would end her obsession with Wagner once and for all.

As Goldhill looked back down at his *Financial Times* in London, the balloon man and his two escorts reached the end of the passenger coach.

The man in front wrenched the rear door open and in the dim light from the corridor the balloon man saw the front of the big hearse at the head of the flat cars. In the rush of air he saw the man ahead step over to the flatcar section and hesitated. He felt something jab him in the back and turned to the man behind him.

The balloon man snarled above the clattering of the train, "What the hell's this? What kind of place is this for the Swiss cops to take me?"

The eyes under the fedora stared expressionlessly back at him.

"If you believe I'm a Swiss cop, you'll believe what I'm sticking in your back right now is a banana. Now move, Johnny Quaranta."

The man who had killed Sir Harry Oakes felt a sudden sickening lurch in his stomach as the man in front reached back and dragged him across to the flatcar.

Both gunmen crowded him along the side of the

248

hearse and shoved him in the back seat just in front of the coffin as one of the hearse drivers opened the door.

The door slammed, and inside, in the dark, the noise of the train abated slightly.

Between the two men Johnny Quaranta started shaking.

The man in the fedora said, "Trombetta's been looking for you for a long, long time, Johnny."

Quaranta tried one last time.

"Look, fellas, I don't know who you think I am, but my name's Alfred Kent. I've just been in more trouble than you'd ever know and I don't want any more."

The second gunman spoke as the two hearse drivers sat silently in front, staring straight ahead in the dark.

"We know all about your troubles. So does Trombetta. He saw your picture all over the American papers when they mistook you for that Kraut. And Johnny, don't bother to lie to us any more. We checked that fingerprint from Guatemala and United Fruit with the one the cops took off you in Rome."

He tapped the balloon man on the chest.

"Don't forget it was Trombetta fixed you up with that phony passport in the name of Kent."

The balloon man felt the blood drain from his face and his heart began to pound.

"O.K., so I am Quaranta. But for Chrissake, guys, that was more than thirty years ago. Give me a break. I've still got the ten grand in a bank here. I'll give it back to Trombetta. I'll give it to you guys, and you can say you never found me."

"No way," grunted the man in the fedora. "You took Trombetta's money and you loused up the job and cost him lots more straightening it all out. And you chickened out when Trombetta sent for you. You know the rules."

Quaranta was whining now. "No, no, you can't do

that. I left a note in a bank saying it would be Trombetta if I'm found dead."

The second gunman laughed harshly.

"Who said anything about finding you dead, Johnny? We just wanted to give you a little present from Trombetta."

He leaned over with a gloved hand and shoved somthing at Quaranta in the dark. "Put it in your pocket," said the gunman.

Quaranta's clammy, shaking hand grabbed at the object and he recoiled sharply as a thorn bit into his palm.

In the dark he didn't need to peer down. He knew the rules.

His last thought was, "A prickly pear—we always used to stick it in the wallet pocket of a man who stole Mafia money."

More than thirty years later Quaranta paid the debt in full as a thin cord dropped round his neck and tightened. The sixty-seven year old man's sallow features became puce as he thrashed around with his hands and feet, a black-gloved hand shoved his head back and the cord became the last thing he ever felt.

To this day Quaranta's confession to the murder of Sir Harry Oakes still lies in a vault at the Banco della Mercede in Rome, the safekeeping charges being duly deducted by the bank from the monthly interest still sent him by the Swiss Bank Corporation in Zurich.

Because no one knows he is dead.

Within seconds of his last convulsion the hearse drivers and the two gunmen had clambered out to the back of the car and turned the coffin upside down. It was a very special kind, made only in Sicily, where the Mafia controls all the funeral parlors. It was very deep, and when the men prised the bottom off there was a compartment just big enough to cram Quaranta's body inside. The men from the island of the split-level coffin had time to hammer the bottom back on, turn it back up the right way and sit back in the hearse and the back-up car with two minutes to spare before the train thundered out of the Simplon into the bright sun.

That afternoon in Geneva the Swiss banker and mourners who attended the funeral of his dear departed wife would have been surprised to know he had got two burials for the price of one.

But then, if a Swiss banker can't get a bargain, who can?

MY FIRST
Peggy Aldrich
Men and women from all walks discuss their first sexual experiences.
LB 355KK $1.75

GENERATION OF BLOOD
I.A. Grenville
In the tradition of Mandingo—a slave who frees himself from his masters and emotions.
LB 340ZK $1.25

THE CULT OF KILLERS
Donald MacIvers
Worse than Helter Skelter and the Manson Family . . . crazed killers loose in California.
LB 364DK $1.50

HURRICANE
Gardner Fox
Disaster! A wild hurricane sweeps down on a summer resort forcing its inhabitants to face themselves . . . and death!
LB 375DK $1.50

MERCENARY: GREEN HELL
Leon DaSilva
The story of an American mercenary inside the provisional IRA.
LB 388DK $1.50

SEND TO: LEISURE BOOK
P.O. Box 270
Norwalk, Connecticut 06852

Please send me the following titles:

Quantity	Book Number	Price
_____	_____	_____
_____	_____	_____
_____	_____	_____
_____	_____	_____
_____	_____	_____

In the event we are out of stock on any of your selections, please list alternate titles below.

_____	_____	_____
_____	_____	_____
_____	_____	_____
_____	_____	_____

Postage/Handling _____

I enclose . . . . . . _____

FOR U.S. ORDERS. add 35¢ per book to cover cost of postage and handling. Buy five or more copies and we will pay for shipping. Sorry no C.O.D.'s.

FOR ORDERS SENT OUTSIDE THE U.S.A.
Add $1.00 for the first book and 25¢ for each additional book. PAY BY foreign draft or money order drawn on a U.S. bank, payable in U.S. ($) dollars.

☐ Please send me a free catalog.

NAME_____
(Please print)

ADDRESS_____

CITY _____ STATE _____ ZIP _____
Allow Four Weeks for Delivery